COUNTERING
HIS CLAIM

For Amelia.
For all the fun and love you bring.

One

With a final, fond look at the Melbourne skyline, Della Walsh stepped onto the boarding bridge of the *Cora Mae,* the luxury cruise liner she called home.

Ahead on the deck, she spotted a group of people in business suits clustered around a tall man with his back to her. She hesitated, assessing the crowd. All she could see of the man in the center was broad shoulders encased in a tailored business jacket, a straight confident bearing and hair of darkest blond that tapered in against his neck. But that was enough to draw her attention and keep it there. The ship's captain stood beside him and from various vantage points, beyond the grand foyer, groups of curious staff intently watched the interaction.

Which meant, most likely, the man in the middle of the action was *him.*

Luke Marlow, the man about to inherit the *Cora Mae,* had arrived.

Curiosity nibbling, she stepped into the foyer. Many senior crew members, including herself, had been invited to the reading of Patrick Marlow's will today, and all of them had one question uppermost in their minds—what would his nephew and heir, Luke Marlow, do with the ship once he had control? Sell? Refurbish? Interfere with the day-to-day running?

Della was probably more interested in their guest than most—she'd been hearing snippets of Luke's life from Patrick for years. It was possible she knew more about this man than she knew about some of her friends.

As she drew closer to the small crowd, she could hear Captain Tynan say, "We'll get that cut seen to straight away."

Luke Marlow held up a hand wrapped in what looked like a blue handkerchief. "No need. I'll run it under the tap and throw on a bandage."

The captain spotted Della. "Dr. Walsh! Good timing. Mr. Marlow has a cut that might need a couple of stitches."

She pasted a smile on her face, and stepped forward, prepared to offer medical assistance as if he was any other patient, not the man who would soon be her boss. "Good afternoon, Mr. Marlow. If you'll follow me to the medical suite, we'll take a look at your hand."

As she spoke, Luke Marlow slowly turned to her, his steel-gray gaze scanning her face before coming to land on her eyes. The air seemed to sizzle and spark; a wave of goose bumps rushed across her skin. Was she nervous because he held her future in the palm of his hand? Or was it his fallen angel's face—sculpted cheekbones, strong straight nose and sensual lips—that unsettled her? Whatever it was, the effect was unwelcome and she squashed it.

"Now that you mention it," he said thoughtfully, his

eyes not wavering from hers, "I think it might need stitches."

The captain nodded, satisfied. "I'll take care of your staff and a purser will collect you from Dr. Walsh's office and bring you to us when you're done."

As if in slow motion, the crowd parted and Luke Marlow covered the distance between them. He stood within touching distance, looking at her expectantly, and her heart thumped hard and erratically. Tall and charismatic, he filled her vision, making her breath come too fast, as if casting a spell over her....

Her smile slipped. This couldn't be happening. She'd vowed never to let herself feel attraction to a man again. Ever. And *this* man was about to become her boss. Perhaps determine her future. Refusing to give in to her body's blind response, she pulled herself to her full height—which leveled out in the vicinity of Luke's chin—and found that professional smile again.

"This way," she said, indicating the direction with her hand.

Luke inclined his head and stepped away from the dissipating crowd. When they walked farther into the foyer with its elaborate furnishings and chandeliers, she wondered if he noticed the eyes following him from every direction.

"Tell me something, Dr. Walsh," he said, his voice pitched somewhere between sexy-low and curiosity.

Steeling herself against the shiver that threatened to run down her spine at the timbre of his voice, she led him through the foyer, to the bank of elevators. "If I can."

"Is there always a group that size waiting to greet guests?"

The elevator arrived and after they stepped in, she

pressed the button for the third deck. "No, but then you're not an average guest."

He arched an eyebrow several shades darker than his hair. "What sort of guest am I?"

The only guest who's made my knees go weak. She paused for a long moment. He wasn't merely the only guest who'd affected her this strongly, he was the only *man* who had since... She shied away from the thought and schooled her features into casual ambivalence. "We've heard you'll likely inherit the *Cora Mae* today."

"Ah," he said and sank his good hand into his pocket.

He'd thought they wouldn't know? Patrick Marlow had made no secret over the years that he considered his nephew his heir. "Rumors travel quickly around a ship."

"Rumors?" That eyebrow rose again. "There's more than one?"

Three hundred and thirty people lived and worked on the *Cora Mae*. Some were seasonal staff who wanted to see the world. They tended to work hard and party harder. But there was a solid core of people who did more than merely live on board—they'd formed a community. This ship was their home. And both groups were alive with speculation and snippets of information about Luke Marlow. Patrick had often spoken to her about his only nephew, mentioning his privileged background, his success with Marlow Hotels and the respect he garnered in the business world. But those stories from a proud uncle hadn't prepared her for the toe-curling effect Luke had in person.

The elevator doors slid open and she led the way down a narrow, carpeted corridor while the man in question waited patiently for his answer. "Several rumors," she acknowledged, "most of which probably have no basis in fact."

"Humor me."

She allowed herself a small smile at the idea of telling the man who would soon control both her career and home about the gossip doing the rounds. "I don't think so."

They arrived at the medical suite and Della stopped at the reception desk just inside the door to speak to the duty nurse. "Jody, is Dr. Bateman in?"

Something about Luke Marlow affected her. Perhaps it was his power over her future as her boss. Or the strange magnetism he had as a man. Or simply her unsettled nerves about the reading of Patrick's will in an hour and the accompanying sharp reminder of her friend's death only twelve days ago. Regardless, she knew if she didn't feel 100 percent comfortable, it would be more appropriate to hand him to a colleague for treatment.

Hearing his name, Cal Bateman stepped into the reception room and Della's shoulders loosened in relief.

"Cal, Mr. Marlow might need some sutures in his hand." She turned to their patient. "Dr. Bateman will take care of you."

But when she turned to go, Luke's smooth, deep voice stopped her. "No."

Her heart skipped a beat and she swiveled slowly back around. "Pardon?"

Luke stood facing her, dominating the room with his height and presence, his expression neither stern nor encouraging. "If I need stitches, I'd like you to handle them, Dr. Walsh."

Puzzled, she looked at him. Why should it matter to him which doctor he saw? "I assure you, Dr. Bateman's surgical skills are second to none. He did some advanced training in plastic surgery, so he'll leave less of a scar than I would."

"I don't mind a scar," Luke said, unconcerned. "I want you, Dr. Walsh."

Her chest tightened. Was he flirting with her? No man had tried since…her husband. She deliberately cultivated an unapproachable aura to prevent it. Though, Luke Marlow didn't seem the sort of man who bothered taking notice of such things. She held back a sigh. Either way, it didn't matter. She was a professional. She'd treat Patrick's nephew, a man who made her pulse jump, and she'd do a good job of it.

"Of course," she said. She led him into her consulting room and began collecting the supplies she'd need. "Take a seat over here, please, Mr. Marlow."

"Luke," he said and sank into the patient chair.

"I'd rather keep to Mr. Marlow if it's all the same to you." She took her white coat from the hook behind the door and thrust her arms through the sleeves before turning back to him. "Chances are you'll be my boss in a few hours."

"It's not all the same to me. You're about to pierce my skin with a sharp needle and I'd feel more comfortable if we moved past formalities."

Della regarded him for a moment as he stretched out in the black vinyl chair, shoulders relaxed. He wasn't nervous, sutures or no sutures. But since he'd be inheriting the *Cora Mae,* he called the shots. She nodded once. "Luke, then."

He looked at the badge attached to her white coat. "Dr. Adele Walsh," he read. "Can I call you Adele?"

She held back the flinch. Only her husband had called her Adele. An image of Shane's dear face rose up in her mind, threatening to overwhelm her. She focused on Luke. "I prefer Della."

"Della." He blinked languidly as he regarded her. "I

like it. Now that we're on more intimate footing, tell me what the other rumors are."

Before she could restrain it, a chuckle escaped at the way he'd maneuvered. "Well played, *Luke*." She leaned back on the sink and folded her arms under her breasts. "Do you really want to waste time here talking about rumors?"

He met her gaze directly, deep gravity in his silver-gray eyes. "I suppose not. But there is something I would like to ask."

For less than an instant, her breathing stalled—she could guess what his question would be about. Still, the topic was bound to be raised sometime; better to have it dealt with before the will reading.

She took a breath and found a reassuring smile. "Ask whatever you'd like."

"We've been told one of the doctors on the ship cared for my uncle through his illness. A woman."

"Yes," she said, her voice not quite steady.

"Was it you?"

A ball of emotion lodged in her throat, so she gave a nod for her reply. Part of her still couldn't believe Patrick was gone. He'd been such a vibrant man, full of personality, and suddenly he wasn't here to chat and joke with. And Patrick's death had brought her grief over losing her husband two years ago back to the surface.

Luke's gaze was steady and solemn. "Thank you for doing that for him."

She swallowed and found her voice. "You're welcome. But there's no need to thank me—I considered Patrick a friend. He deserved the chance to live out his days on the ship instead of ashore in a hospice."

"One thing confuses me. None of his family knew he was dying. He and I spoke several times on the phone over the past few months and he didn't mention it. He used to stay with my mother every three months for a couple of days, and we knew he was too unwell to come recently but no one suspected things were that bad." Elbows resting on the chair's armrests, he steepled his fingers under his chin. "Why didn't we know?"

She thought back to several conversations she'd had with Patrick where she'd suggested he tell his family how serious his cancer was—or closer to the end, that he let her call them. But he'd been adamant. He didn't want them to see him frail and wasted, and he didn't want to endure their reactions to seeing him in that state. He said he wanted them to remember him as he'd been, but she'd wondered if it was denial—if a distraught family had arrived, he would have had to face his own mortality head-on.

She tightened her crossed arms a little. "Patrick was a proud man and he thought it would be for the best this way."

"How long was he unwell?" Luke asked quietly.

"He'd had cancer for almost a year, and he'd been ashore for two rounds of chemotherapy, but it became more serious about four months ago. Even then, he was still mobile and involved with the running of the ship until about three weeks before he died."

"Was he in any—" he frowned and seemed to think better of the word "—much pain?"

"I administered morphine and other medications as required, so his discomfort was minimal." On occasions she'd even had to convince him to take the pain relief. Patrick had been of the soldier-on mold.

"Was there…" Luke hesitated and ran his good hand through his hair. "I honestly mean no disrespect, but was he seeing any other doctors, as well?"

He needn't have worried; she understood. If their situations had been reversed, she'd ask the same question, want to know that *her* uncle had been given the best possible treatment.

"He was under the care of a specialist at the Royal Sydney Hospital, and I had regular contact with her. I can give you her details if you'd like to talk to her yourself." Luke gave a single shake of his head so she continued. "For the last two months of his life, Patrick personally paid for an extra doctor to take over my regular duties so I could focus solely on him. We also brought a specialist nurse on board so there was someone with him twenty-four hours a day."

Though, even when the nurse had been on duty, Della had found it difficult to leave him, and had checked in often.

Luke nodded his acceptance of the information as he let out a long breath. "Will you be at the will reading?"

"Yes." Patrick had made her promise to attend, saying he'd left her a little something. Telling him he didn't need to had made no difference. "Quite a few of the crew have been invited."

"I hope Patrick left you something for what you did for him, but if he didn't have time to change his will, I'll make sure you receive something of meaning."

With a twinge of grief in her chest, she realized that the generosity in his expression reminded her of Patrick, and of the stories he'd told about the man before her. She'd often wondered if Patrick had exaggerated his stories about his nephew or if Luke really was a prince among men.

"That's sweet of you," she said. "But there's no need. I was doing my job and as I said, I had a lot of respect for Patrick. I counted him as a friend. I wouldn't have had things any other way."

"Either way, I'm grateful you were able to be there for him."

"I appreciate you saying that," she said and meant it. She'd often wondered if Patrick's family would blame her for their not knowing about his illness. "And if you're going to make that will reading, we need to take a look at your cut now."

He glanced down at his watch. "You're right."

She washed her hands, sat down across a table from him and set out the sterile cloth. "Lay your hand over here," she said as she slipped on a pair of gloves.

Luke looked into Dr. Della Walsh's eyes and laid his hand, palm up, on the table. She was an intriguing woman. It couldn't have been easy caring for his stubborn uncle out at sea, yet the information from the ship's captain when he'd rung the family twelve days ago was that Patrick's care had been second to none. But it was something else that had compelled him to insist she handle his stitches— something that radiated from within her. She wore no makeup yet her toffee-brown gaze captivated him more than any preening society woman. Her eyes held depth, intelligence and the promise of something more.

Breaking the eye contact, he frowned. It didn't seem right to think this way about the doctor who'd cared for Patrick until his death, especially when that had been so recent that he could still feel the permanent punch to the gut the loss had created.

Della looked down and gently unwrapped the blue handkerchief he'd tied around his hand. It wasn't much of a cut, more a good-size nick at the base of his thumb, but she was treating it seriously. That made him feel even better about Patrick's care in the past few months.

"I'll just give you some local anesthetic," she said as she

drew up a needle. The two jabs into the fleshy part of his palm stung, but Della's hand, soft and warm through the gloves, stabilized his as she administered the drug. Then she swiped the area with an antiseptic and gave it a quick wash with clear fluid from a bottle marked *sterile saline*.

She bent her head and scanned his palm closely. "How did you do it?"

"Car accident."

Her eyes flew to his, then roved down his neck, across his shoulders, assessing everywhere she could see. "Are you hurt anywhere else? And the others in the car with you?"

"We're all fine," he said with a casual shrug. "To be fair, you could hardly class it as an accident. I was pouring some sparkling water from the minibar into a glass—"

She blinked. "I thought this was in a car?"

"Stretch limo." He'd needed to meet with several of his staff, and hated wasting time traveling, so the price of a larger vehicle to accommodate the meeting was easily worth it. "The driver had to swerve hard in traffic, just hitting the bumper of another car. The glass in my hand caught the corner of the fridge as I swung forward, and it shattered."

"You were lucky," she said, returning her attention to his palm.

The cut was minor, but it had led him here, so perhaps he had been lucky. His gaze was drawn back to the doctor's silky brown hair as she bent her head forward.

"Can you move your thumb for me? And the index finger?"

Obediently, he bent his thumb and finger in turn.

"Okay, good. Tell me if you can feel this."

The featherlight touch of her gloved fingertip ran across the planes of his fingers and thumb. "Yes."

She nodded, satisfied, and picked up a pair of tweezers. "I'm just checking for glass fragments while the anesthetic takes effect. This shouldn't hurt," she murmured.

Her dark lashes swept down over creamy pale cheeks as she worked. Under normal circumstances, he'd have asked her out for a drink, maybe dinner, but that would cross a line now that she would soon be an employee.

Besides, he doubted Della would take him up on the offer. The signals she'd been sending had been limited to professional concern, both for his hand and because he was Patrick's nephew.

She skimmed a finger over a long, straight scar along the length of his thumb pad. "This looks like it would have been a nasty cut."

A faint smile pulled at his mouth. "Childhood accident." Though, it had been far from an accident—it had been with conscious, purposeful intent that, at thirteen, he'd sliced his thumb with a pocketknife and pressed the injury against similar ones on three friends' thumbs. They'd become blood brothers that night in a darkened boarding school dorm room. He looked at the scar, remembering how his youthful enthusiasm had made him slash long and deep—as though more blood would deepen the bond. Maybe it had, because he was still closer to those guys than any other person on the planet.

Della put the tweezers down, then picked up the needle.

"How does it look?" he asked.

"It's only minor," she said, all polite reassurance. The needle pierced his skin and he felt a slight tugging as she sewed the stitch. Della worked quickly and efficiently after the first one was in place, knotting and cutting. Her hands as they worked were graceful and capable, like Della herself.

After she tied off the third one, she rose and removed

her gloves, saying over her shoulder, "Have you had a tetanus shot recently?"

"About a year ago."

"That will be fine. You shouldn't need antibiotics—the cut was clean, and there was no foreign material." She washed her hands then turned back to him. "You'll need the stitches out in about seven days. If you're still here, come to the clinic and either Cal or I will do it. If you've left by then, see your local doctor."

A twinge of regret surprised him. "I'm only here for a couple of nights." He'd come for the reading of Patrick's will and to spend a few days assessing the ship's operations. He'd disembark when they reached Sydney.

"You're not staying for a full run?" A fine line appeared between her eyebrows. "To experience the *Cora Mae* out in the Pacific?"

"That won't be necessary." His plans for the ship didn't include her cruising the Pacific or anywhere.

"Then you'll need to see your own doctor in a week, Mr. Marlow," she said with her courteous, professional smile. "Ring him earlier if you have any concerns or your hand shows signs of unusual pain, redness or swelling."

With a start, he realized the appointment was over. He was seconds away from walking out the door and in all probability wouldn't see her one-on-one again. Which was probably for the best—that impulse he'd had to invite her for a drink might reemerge, and he wouldn't start anything with a future employee who never spent more than one night in any given city.

He nodded, and rested a hand on the doorknob. "Thank you for the medical care, Dr. Walsh. I appreciate it."

"You're welcome, Mr. Marlow," she said, her voice even, unaffected.

Something about this woman intrigued him, and that was rare. What if, despite the obstacles—

Walk away now, the sane part of his brain said. *This is not a woman for you.* Which was true. He shook his head ruefully and stepped through the door, only just reining in the impulse to turn back for one final look over his shoulder at Dr. Della Walsh.

Two

Less than an hour later, Della rushed along a carpeted corridor to the boardroom where Patrick Marlow's will was probably already being read. She hated being late. Hated it. Being late meant drawing attention to herself and that made her uncomfortable anytime. And this was such an important occasion.

The life of a shipboard doctor wasn't frantic like a medical career based in a hospital, but occasionally there would be a run of patients. Just after Luke had left the clinic, they'd had a minor influx of passengers returning early from shore—a child with a bee sting, another with a twisted wrist after a fall, a young woman with a migraine and a man with a bad case of sunburn. She couldn't have left them all to Cal.

She flicked a glance at her watch. Only three minutes past two—hopefully people were still taking their seats.

Arriving late to Patrick's will reading seemed disrespectful, and the thought made her skin prickle.

Gently pushing open the door, she let out a breath—although people were seated, there was still murmuring as the short, gray-haired man at the front table shuffled papers on his desk. Most chairs were taken, but she was relieved to see a vacant aisle seat in the back row. She slipped in and greeted the woman beside her.

"Have I missed anything?" Della whispered.

"No," Jackie said. "He just asked everyone to take their seats. It's a bit surreal, isn't it? I still can't believe Patrick's gone, let alone that we're all sitting around to talk about his money." Jackie ran the housekeeping department and had been friends with the ship's owner, as had many of the senior staff.

Tears stung the back of her eyes but Della blinked them away. "Even knowing how sick he was at the end, part of me kept believing he'd pull through."

"Well, *he* thought he'd pull through," Jackie said, shaking her head, her smile a bittersweet mix of admiration and sadness. "He was still making plans the last time I saw him."

Breath tight in her lungs, Della had to pause before her voice would work. "Determination and optimism were probably what kept him going longer than his specialists expected."

"You were a big part of that, too, Della." Jackie took her hand and squeezed, and Della appreciated the warmth, the solidarity. "We all know the long hours you put in with him, going above and beyond. The way you devoted yourself to making sure he was as comfortable as he could be. And Patrick knew it, too. He sang your praises whenever he could, told us he was indebted to you."

Della managed something of a crooked smile, but this

time her constricted chest wouldn't let her reply. Thankfully, the man at the front of the room cleared his throat and introduced himself as Patrick Marlow's lawyer and executor of his will.

As he spoke, Della's gaze drifted to Luke Marlow, also in an aisle seat, but in the front row beside the captain. His back was tall and straight in the chair and, just as when she'd first seen him when she was boarding a few hours ago, she found it difficult to drag her attention away. There was something magnetic about that man.

Then he slowly turned and searched the crowd before his gaze landed on her. A shiver of tingles ran down her spine. His head dipped in acknowledgment, and she nodded back, before he turned to the front again. Della tucked a curl behind her ear and tried to put Luke Marlow from her mind as best she could. She was here for Patrick.

The executor had finished his preamble and come to the division of assets. He'd left a collection of rare and first edition books to his sister-in-law, Luke's mother, who, the executor noted, hadn't been able to attend; he left some personal effects such as cuff links and a tie clip to various members of staff.

"Regarding the ownership of the cruise ship, the *Cora Mae*..." The executor paused for a muffled cough and darted a quick glance around. "I leave a one-half share to my nephew, Luke Marlow."

The room was silent for the longest beat as though everyone was too shocked to move. Then a wave of murmuring washed over the small crowd.

Luke had inherited *one half*? As Della struggled to make sense of the phrase, her gaze flew to Luke. He sat very straight, very still.

One half meant...there was someone else. She could feel the sudden wariness of every crew member present—

if their future had seemed uncertain five minutes ago, it was now even more unpredictable. She ran through Patrick's stories of his family in her mind for possibilities, scanned the rigid bodies sitting in the front row. Although their tension was nothing compared to that emanating from Luke as he sat motionless, waiting, focused.

"The other one-half share," the executor continued, "I leave to Dr. Della Walsh."

What? Her heart skidded to a halt then leaped to life again, thumping hard in her chest, each beat a painful hammer in her ears. *Oh, God.*

Surely there was a mistake. She replayed the words in her head, looking for where she'd misunderstood, but found nothing. What had Patrick done?

People turned in their seats to face her, some with mouths open, others with confused frowns, a few whispering her name in incredulous voices.

Even through the bewilderment, the irony struck her— despite rushing and managing to arrive before the proceedings had begun, every pair of eyes in the room was on her, after all. A bubble of hysterical laughter rose up, then died again when Luke pinned her with fierce gray eyes.

She leaned back against the chair, away from the force of his unspoken accusation. Abruptly, he stood and the crowd's attention switched to him. Her skin went cold as he stalked down the aisle then stopped to loom over her.

"Dr. Walsh," he said through a tight jaw. "A word in private, if you please."

He held his hand out, plainly expecting her to rise and precede him out of the room. Her jellied joints felt unequal to the task but after a moment she managed to force herself to her feet. As she swiveled, she nearly stumbled. A firm warm grip encircled her elbow, steadying her, saving her from that ignominy.

She turned to thank him but her throat seized as she met the hard glitter in his eyes. Her stomach flipped. With all the grace she could muster, she allowed him to guide her out to the corridor.

Once the door to the boardroom had shut behind them, he looked from closed door to closed door. "An empty room where we can talk undisturbed?"

Willing her brain to work, she indicated the door on the left and he headed for it, still gripping her elbow. It was smaller than the room they'd come from, designed for meetings of no more than ten people, furnished with a rectangular table surrounded by chairs and one porthole.

As soon as the door clicked closed, Luke released her and his hands moved to his hips, suspicion and anger radiating from every inch of his six-foot-plus frame.

"Tell me something, Dr. Walsh," he said, his voice harsh and a sneer curling his top lip. "What exactly did you do for my uncle to earn yourself half a ship?"

It took a moment but then his meaning slammed into her. He thought she'd used her body, sold herself to manipulate sweet, lovely Patrick for financial gain. Rage charged through her veins, hot and wild. Before she'd even realized her intention, her hand was swinging toward him. His eyes widened. He began to turn away, but it was too late.

A crack echoed as flesh met flesh. The force of her slap jerked his head sideways. Heat and pain streaked across her palm, leaving the rest of her body icy cold, and the jolt shuddered all the way up her arm to her shoulder.

And then she froze. She'd struck another human being in anger. The violence felt ugly, alien…she felt alien. She looked down at her upturned palm. Warily her gaze crept up to Luke's face, to the red imprint of her hand on his cheek and a wave of nausea cramped her stomach.

* * *

Luke swore under his breath. He'd never been slapped before. Now that he had, it wasn't an experience he wanted to repeat in a hurry. His cheek hurt like hell.

Della's hand still hung in the air as if she didn't know what to do with it now. Her face was blanched of color. Whatever else he may think of her, he could see the slap was out of character. Not that it mattered. What mattered more was that he'd lost his temper. If he were to succeed, control would be his friend. Control over himself, leading to control of the situation. No more angry outbursts—a cool head would win the day.

He spun away and strode over to the other end of the room, trying to find his bearings. He glanced up at a framed photo on the wall of the original *Cora Mae* proudly entering Sydney Harbour over fifty years ago. Patrick's *Cora Mae* had been named after the ship in the photo, which had been Luke's grandfather's, and that ship had been named for Luke's grandmother, Cora Mae Marlow. Now he was effectively sharing his heritage with a stranger…at least until he could rectify the situation. A heaviness pressed down on his shoulders.

What had Patrick been *thinking* to put him in this position? He scraped both hands through his hair and blew out a breath.

"I have to know," he said, still facing the photo of the *Cora Mae*. "When we met earlier and you stitched my hand. Were you aware then that Patrick was leaving you half the ship?"

He turned to face Della. She'd slipped into a chair, her head was bowed, her hands in her lap—her left hand held her right wrist as though she was afraid of what it might do next. Those were the long slender fingers that had stitched his wound with such dexterity, such tenderness. Who'd have thought they'd be capable of delivering such a stinging rebuke.

"No." Her gaze didn't waver. "I had no idea."

He surveyed her, curling his fingers around the top of the chair, feeling the padding give under his fingertips. She was the doctor who'd nursed Patrick through his final illness, when he'd been at his most vulnerable. Had she used that time to sway him? To garner a financial reward? Perhaps exerted subtle—or not so subtle—influence over a susceptible, sick man?

He released the chair, dug his uninjured hand into his pocket and rocked back on his heels. "It's a pretty big gift to be a surprise."

"Patrick had said on more than one occasion that he was grateful I'd arranged for him to be cared for on the *Cora Mae.* The ship was his home and he was afraid he wouldn't be able to stay here. Which was why he tried to hide his symptoms as long as he could." Her eyes closed tight for a long moment, and when she opened them again, she focused on the ceiling. "He also said he'd leave me 'a little something' in his will."

Luke let his silence ask the questions.

She folded her arms under her breasts. "I told him it was unnecessary, that I was just doing my job."

"But you did more than your job, didn't you?" he asked softly. "You were with him almost constantly."

"Yes." Her eyes flashed but her voice was even and calm. "I loved Patrick and I would have done anything for him. I know what you're implying but I didn't care for him for any reward. He was part of my onboard family as well as a mentor and a friend."

Luke paced across to the porthole, giving himself a few moments to regroup. Patrick was *her* family and her friend?

Why hadn't his uncle asked for him? He'd have dropped everything in an instant if he'd known Patrick was so seriously ill. He'd have wanted to be at the old man's side, wouldn't have cared that he was frail or tired or any of the other things that the illness had caused. He just wished he'd been there, to talk to him, to hold his hand, to watch over him. A hot ball of emotion lodged in his throat.

Was this part of his problem with Della? She *had* been here, she had talked to Patrick, helped him, perhaps comforted him in his hours of need. Her competence had provided succor, and Luke wished he'd been a part of that care. It made his voice harsher than he'd intended.

"He was a *friend* with the capacity to make you a rich woman."

"Challenge the bloody will, then." She looked glorious in her anger, her dark eyes shining bright and color high on her cheeks. "Drag it through the courts. Make it look like Patrick wasn't of sound mind. Knock yourself out."

Her angry words brought him up short. It would go against the grain to tarnish Patrick's memory by publically claiming his uncle was incompetent. But he might not have a choice. This was his heritage—how could he just let that go?

The silence was thick and heavy, and when a knock came at the door, it startled him back to the surroundings.

Della turned and wrenched open the door. A crew member stood on the other side. "The executor would like Mr. Marlow back in the room. He's outlining personal effects, so I expect you'll be mentioned again."

Luke nodded then turned to Della. "This conversation isn't over."

"I look forward to continuing it," she said, and stalked from the room.

He watched her leave—the movement of her hips under the soft fabric of her trousers, the bounce of her dark curls at her shoulders—and shook his head. Wasn't this going to make it hell for negotiating? The last thing he needed was this simmering desire, this spark with his uncle's doctor—and the part-owner of Luke's ship. He'd already paid the price of handling her with uncontrolled emotion. A stinging slap and the knowledge that his fierce self-discipline was not as unassailable as he'd believed.

Next time they met, his control over his temper and his body would once again be ironclad.

Della sat in the back row for the remainder of the will reading, listening to various possessions being allocated to family as well as crew members who had been treasured friends. Although she tried to prevent it, her gaze kept straying to Luke Marlow, his accusations replaying in her mind. The first—that she'd been more than a doctor to Patrick—still sat in the air like a blight on Patrick's memory. And the second—that she'd somehow influenced Patrick to leave her half the ship when he was in a vulnerable state—was abhorrent. But admittedly, Luke didn't know her well enough to know she could never stoop to doing something like that. Which didn't stop the insult from eating at her gut like acid.

There was an aura of restrained tension in and around Luke's body as he sat facing the front. Others may not notice, but she'd been watching him before the executor had announced that Patrick had left them half the ship each and there was a definite difference in the set of his shoulders now. She could imagine he was probably grinding his teeth, as well. Life had probably come so easily to him—born into a wealthy family, having the advantages of looks, charm and intelligence—that being disappointed like this was likely a new experience. Luke and disappointment probably hadn't even been on speaking terms until now.

But that wasn't her problem. And if he wanted to challenge the will in court, so be it. Patrick had been lucid until the last couple of days and there was a large group of people on board who'd be able to testify to that. She might not have been expecting to be left a gift this size, but neither was she about to throw it away simply because a rich man was used to getting his own way. She needed time to think about it all, to let it settle in her mind.

As the executor wound up and said he'd be in touch again with all the beneficiaries, Della sneaked out the door. She wasn't in the frame of mind to deal with the questions and comments from the crew, or for Luke to pick up their unfinished conversation.

Temples pounding, she hurried down the corridors until she reached her cabin. After a cup of coffee and half an hour to catch her breath, she rang her parents to see if they'd known of Patrick's intentions. Despite her father becoming close friends with Patrick while he was captain of the *Cora Mae,* they were as surprised as she, but they were thrilled.

She skipped lunch, her stomach in too many knots for food, and sat staring out her porthole, playing the morning's events over in her mind. By dinnertime, she hadn't come to any conclusions, but knew one thing. She had to face the ship. There was no doubt that this would be the hot topic of gossip and the thought made her cringe, but she refused to hide out. The captain was expecting her at his table tonight. She dressed for dinner in her favorite teal satin dress, which always made her feel good—but it would have a tough job tonight.

One final deep breath before she opened the door, ready to face the questions that were surely coming. Face the stares. Face the man.

Luke sat at the captain's table, engaging in small talk with the captain to his left, but most of his attention was on scanning the crowd for Della Walsh. He'd spent the afternoon trying to track her down. First stop had been the medical suite but she hadn't been on duty and the staff had been protective, refusing to give out her details. In fact, wherever he'd tried, he'd come up against a brick wall—the crew of the *Cora Mae* were like a shield around their doctor. But the captain had told him Della was expected at dinner tonight and she'd never missed dinner at his table when she was expected. So Luke had arrived early and bided his time. He would talk to Dr. Walsh about Patrick's will tonight.

His gaze flitted from person to person, taking in the suited men, the women in richly colored evening gowns, the sparkling jewelry. Then he saw her weaving her way around the tables and his heart skidded to a halt. The fabric of her dress caught the light from the chandeliers and shimmered, her brown hair in soft waves on her shoulders. Her dark eyes met his for a sweet moment before her attention was snared by a woman at her elbow. Beautiful was such an inadequate word.

He stared at her for a full five seconds after she looked away, only vaguely aware of whatever the captain was saying beside him. Then he pulled himself up. He'd met a lot of attractive women in his life—some he'd dated, some he'd merely admired, one he'd married. But he had a golden rule: *never be distracted by a woman; never rely on anyone.*

Aside from his disastrous marriage, he'd managed to live his life pretty much according to that rule. The only exception was for his three friends—the blood brothers he'd made at boarding school, where he'd made the cut in his thumb that Della had noticed when she'd done his stitches. He still saw them regularly, particularly to play billiards, but even with them he'd always managed to keep part of himself hidden. Safe.

He wasn't in danger of breaking the second part of his golden rule—to never rely on anyone—with the ship's doctor. But it seemed he might need to watch himself in terms of being distracted by Della Walsh.

He'd admired her this morning when she'd done his stitches, but watching her now as she came another few steps closer before she was waylaid again, his reaction was stronger. Deeper. Perhaps it was seeing her in an evening dress. Perhaps he was more keenly attuned to her since the will reading. Whatever it was, he would not be distracted from the pressing issue: the unresolved questions involving ownership of the *Cora Mae*.

Della finally made it to their table, and an usher seated her in the vacant seat to Luke's right.

"Good evening, Dr. Walsh," he said.

She raised an eyebrow, obviously noting his use of her title after making a fuss about using first names in her medical suite. But he needed to remind himself that they were now locked in a business situation. He wouldn't jeopardize the future of his family's assets over a beautiful woman. He'd learned that lesson already and wasn't in a rush to repeat it.

Luckily, when his ex-wife had taken him to the cleaners, his father had still been alive and Luke had yet to inherit the family business. If he'd been blind to Jillian's machinations for another year or two, the outcome would have been much worse.

Della shook out her napkin and laid it across her lap. "Good evening, Mr. Marlow."

"I hope you had a pleasant afternoon. Unfortunately, I had no luck locating you to continue our discussion."

"I'm sorry to hear that," she said pleasantly enough, but it was clear she wasn't sorry in the least. "How fortunate that you're on a cruise ship equipped with many ways to fill your afternoon."

Before he could reply a middle-aged man in the crisp white uniform that indicated his senior crew member status stopped at Della's shoulder. "Della, I was so pleased when I heard the outcome of Patrick's will. We're all so glad for you."

"Thank you, Colin." Her chin lifted ever so slightly, as if she was meeting a challenge. "I appreciate it."

He glanced at Luke, as if remembering he was there. "And you, too, Mr. Marlow."

"Thank you," Luke said. But he'd caught the undercurrent—the crew was pleased that one of their own had inherited a share of their home and workplace. Understandable, even if the situation wouldn't stand like this for long.

Colin turned back to Della. "You'll be resigning your post as doctor, I assume."

"I haven't made any decisions yet," she said calmly. "Besides, I wouldn't want to leave Dr. Bateman in the lurch."

The man laid a hand on her shoulder and gave a friendly squeeze before moving along. Uncomfortably aware that he hadn't liked seeing another man's hands on Della's bare flesh, Luke watched her over the rim of his wineglass as she straightened the cutlery beside her plate. She'd changed when the man had said he was happy for her. And now a woman sitting two seats farther along than Della leaned over and congratulated her, and again, Della seemed uncomfortable. Almost as if her colleagues being happy for her made her nervous. Interesting.

When Della turned back, Luke laid a hand over her forearm to ensure her attention wouldn't be stolen this time. She glanced up, as if startled by the touch, but he left his hand on the warmth of her skin. "We need to talk. To finish the conversation we started earlier."

Her tongue darted out to moisten her lips. "I know."

A man hovered at Della's shoulder and she began to turn, but Luke tightened his grip on her forearm to a firm but gentle hold. Della held his gaze and the man stepped away.

"We can't talk privately here," Luke said. "As soon as dinner is over we'll go somewhere where no one can interrupt." He glanced around at the people nearby who were subtly—or not so subtly—watching them. "Or eavesdrop."

She scanned his face for long moments before nodding. "I know a place."

"Good," he said and turned to face the table again. "As soon as we've finished eating, you'll take me there."

He'd prefer to go at once, but was prepared to be civilized. And it was better for the crew to see them handling this in a calm manner. Skittish crew members would spook the passengers.

As would a challenge to Patrick's will through the courts. Which was why he'd prefer to resolve this as quickly and as privately as possible. Of course, if he couldn't obtain the outcome he wanted privately with Della, a legal challenge was still plan B.

Della smiled at an older couple taking their seats on her other side. "Welcome back, Mr. Flack, Mrs. Flack."

She turned back to Luke. "Mr. Marlow, this is Mr. and Mrs. Flack. They're regular patrons of the *Cora Mae*."

Mr. Flack leaned across to shake Luke's hand while his wife said, "Lovely to meet you, Mr. Marlow."

Luke stood and reached down in front of Della to shake the guests' hands, an action that gave him a burst of her perfume, a brush of her arm. He refused to let it affect him, and took his seat again.

The wine waiters came and delivered their drinks, and soon all ten seats at the table had filled and Captain Tynan led the conversation among the group. He was obviously an old hand at this, and it gave Luke an opportunity to observe Della some more. Preparation was the key to any confrontation, and he had a lot riding on their meeting after dinner.

After the waiter had taken their meal orders, the main conversation trailed off and Luke turned to Della. "Tell me about yourself."

She took a sip of her wine before answering. "You didn't come to dinner to talk about me. How are you finding your cabin?"

Luke toyed with the stem of his glass as he watched her. In some ways, Della reminded him of a cat—detached and ready to turn and walk away at the slightest provocation. What would make a professional, independent woman like Della feel that way? Was it the conflict with him over the *Cora Mae,* or her reaction to him personally? It was an intriguing question. But he allowed the change of subject to pass without comment.

"Surprisingly comfortable," he said and leaned back in his chair. The duplex suite they'd been able to find him at short notice was much more spacious and luxurious than the cruise ships of his childhood. Ships had come a long way in twenty-five years, or at least his uncle's had. "To be honest, I'm a little surprised at the high standard."

"The *Cora Mae* is a luxury cruise liner. Our guests expect nothing less than absolute quality." She tilted her head to indicate the expansive dining room, decorated in opulent whites and sparkling crystal, its walls draped in lilac gauzy fabric. In the soft glow of the room's light, she was breathtaking. His pulse picked up speed. She wore a simple teal evening gown and the lightest of makeup, her nut-brown hair hanging in loose, shiny curls. Yet, for all her understatement, there was a magnetic charge that surrounded her.

He cleared his throat. "Have you had a busy time in the medical rooms since I was there?"

"I was only on duty until the will reading, so there wasn't too much," she said, absently wiping a finger through the condensation on the side of her glass.

"No other stitches?"

One side of her mouth pulled into a reluctant smile. "You were the only one. After you left I saw a case of sunburn, a twisted wrist from a fall over a mat and one child with a bee sting."

"Was the mat on the ship?" he asked casually, words like liability and lawsuit flashing through his mind.

She shook her head. "A guest who'd been ashore for the day."

He nodded and sipped his wine. He'd only just inherited the ship—well, half the ship—and legal action or other complications weren't the best way to start.

He tipped his glass toward her. "So I was the most interesting patient of the day?"

"You could say that," she conceded with a smile.

"Then I'm glad my suffering was of service," he said

slowly. For a fleeting moment, the veil lifted and awareness flashed in her toffee-brown eyes. Something in that
awareness, in the yearning that lay behind it, called to
him on a primal level, made his blood pump faster, hotter.
His muscles tensed, then she blinked and the expression,
and the moment, were gone. He'd felt a similar pull when
she'd first arrived at the table. There was some chemistry
between them, no denying it. Also no denying that Della
wasn't happy about it.

He'd never had to try too hard with women before—
even Jillian, the wife who'd left him in such grand style,
had practically handed herself to him on a platter. The
fact that Della—despite her attraction to him—would be
more comfortable somewhere else fascinated him more
than he would have predicted.

Their meals arrived and Della was drawn into other
conversations. Luke talked to the captain beside him and
others around the table, but part of his attention remained
on Della, whether he wanted it to or not. He knew when
she took a bite of her roast vegetable salad. Knew when
she touched her mouth with her napkin. Listened to her
gentle laugh. Smelled a faint vanilla fragrance when she
ran her fingers through her hair. And he silently cursed
himself for it. Because in less than an hour, she'd once
again be his opponent.

Three

Della unlocked the door to the ship's library and led the way, flicking on the lights as she went. The room was usually staffed by a crew member for the few hours a day it was open, and outside those times it had become her secret space.

Luke glanced around at the shelves of books and nodded. "Will we be interrupted by people needing a book for nighttime reading?"

"Opening hours are long over. No one will come in until ten tomorrow morning."

He arched an eyebrow. "Is it normal for the ship's doctor to have a key to the library?"

"Not especially," she said and felt the corners of her mouth tug into a smile. "My father used to be captain of this ship, and he gave me the key because he knew how much I loved it in here. I let the new captain know after Dad's retirement and he was happy to leave the arrangement as is."

The librarian had also told the new captain that Della helped keep shelves in order on her frequent visits, so on that point alone he'd been keen to keep her access unfettered. When she couldn't sleep, she liked handling books. Putting them in their proper place. Creating calm and order from chaos. She'd also occasionally bought books when she went ashore and donated them to the library, loving the feeling of being part of this special place.

"Of course," Luke said. "Your father is Dennis Walsh. Patrick mentioned him occasionally."

She wasn't surprised Patrick had mentioned his friend, but she didn't want to discuss her family with Luke Marlow. So she indicated two upholstered armchairs, arranged at right angles to each other, and they sat. Then she waited.

Luke rested an ankle on his knee and steepled his fingers. "I've been thinking. For whatever reason, Patrick wanted to leave you something more than, say, a rare bottle of wine. He didn't have much cash or other assets since most of his wealth was tied up in the *Cora Mae,* so by giving you half the ship, knowing I'd buy you out, he was able to leave you a generous financial gift."

Luke seemed so sure, so confident of himself and his words. It was in the set of his shoulders, the angle of his jaw. She hadn't had that sort of confidence in years— and she certainly didn't have it about Patrick's intentions.

She tilted her head to the side as she studied him. "What makes you think he didn't *want* to leave me half a ship?"

"Patrick's father was Arthur Marlow, my grandfather," he said without hesitation. "He started a company called Marlow and Sons. It owned many ships, including the original *Cora Mae,* which was named after his wife."

She knew the ship's history from Patrick, and had a feeling where Luke was going with this. "There's a portrait of your grandmother hanging in the lobby. I'll show you later if you like."

"Thank you, I'd appreciate that." He nodded in acknowledgment of her offer. "When Arthur died he split the company equally between his two sons. My father sold his ships and bought hotels instead, which he passed to me when he died. Patrick stayed in ships—he started with several but during some lean times, consolidated down to the flagship, the *Cora Mae*. After it became apparent he wouldn't have children of his own, Patrick made it very clear that he wanted to reunite the family company through me."

She leaned back in her chair. There was logic to his story, to his sense of expectation of inheriting, but life didn't always fit into neat boxes, or sit on the shelves in the correct order like the books that surrounded them. Sometimes the unexpected and the irregular were part of life, too. She had no idea what Patrick had been thinking, but he *must* have had some reason for leaving her half a ship. She just had yet to understand his purpose.

"So," she said, choosing her words with care, "because the *Cora Mae* has been in your family, it should simply stay in your family?"

His eyes narrowed. "Cora Mae was my grandmother. We're talking about more than an asset owned by someone I'm related to. This ship is part of the fabric of my family."

"And you think Patrick didn't intend for me to keep the half he gave me?"

"It's the only thing that makes sense." He shrugged his broad shoulders. "I'll buy your half-share and you get the windfall my uncle wanted you to have."

She glanced through the porthole at the moonlight glinting on the rippled surface of the ocean. Allowing

Luke to buy her out was the easiest option, sure, but she wouldn't be railroaded.

"What happens if I don't sell my half to you?" she asked, turning back to him.

"An untenable situation is created. Both of us would have 50 percent so neither would have a controlling interest. We'd have to agree on all major decisions for any real management to happen."

She could see his point, and understood the inherent problems in the current arrangement, but one thought kept floating to the surface—what if Patrick had wanted her to have half the ship for some reason? He'd known how much Della loved the *Cora Mae*. Della had grown up on the ships her parents worked on, and her father had been captain of the *Cora Mae* until his retirement twelve months ago. When he'd offered her a job as a doctor working alongside her mother, she'd jumped at the chance, then spent a year working and cruising with her family. Her mother had retired at the same time as her husband, but Della had stayed. She felt more at home out to sea than she did on land. And the *Cora Mae* was her favorite of the ships she'd lived on, so the sense of ownership she had for the ship probably wouldn't surprise anyone.

She stood and smoothed her hands down her dress. "I'm going to have to think about this, Luke. Selling you my half isn't something I'd do lightly."

In a flash, he was standing beside her. "How about this. Sell me a 10 percent share. I'll pay double its worth, so you'll still end up with a substantial lump sum." He pulled a folded piece of paper from his pocket and handed it to her. "This is the valuation of the ship that I had done a few days ago. Take 10 percent of that bottom figure and double it."

Della felt her eyes widen as she gripped the page. It was more money than she'd dreamed of.

"There will be stability to the management," Luke continued, "and you'll still get to keep your connection to the ship, plus the cash. Everybody wins."

Her breath caught. The idea of having a hand in the future directions of her beloved *Cora Mae,* the promise of the money and the freedom that would bring…it was overwhelming.

Yet, what if Luke was wrong and Patrick had wanted her to have half the ship for some reason? The will reading had only been a few hours ago and in that short time there had already been twists and turns to the situation. It was too much to take in at once.

"I need to think it over." She refolded the page and handed it back to him. Instead of taking it, he enfolded her hand in his, crumpling the paper inside their two sets of fingers and infusing her hand with warmth.

"The longer this draws out, the worse it is for the ship and her crew. They need stability," he said, his voice and eyes both urging her to agree.

Her stomach dipped. So many people would be affected by her decision. But that only made it more imperative that it was the right one.

"I'm sorry, Mr. Marlow," she said, straightening her spine. "This is too big a decision to rush. I'll contact you when I've made up my mind."

He gazed at her for a long time, far from happy. "I won't wait forever," he said, and walked out, leaving her in the library alone.

Thirty-six hours later—thirty-six hours in which he'd neither seen nor heard from Della—Luke walked along a path in the Sydney Botanical Gardens. They'd docked in Sydney that morning, and before he could find her, Della had left the ship. He was out of time and patience, so, after finding out the direction she'd headed in, he'd followed her.

He didn't have the luxury of time to sit around and wait any longer. Even without the mess of Patrick's will to sort out, he had a full-time job running Marlow Hotels. He would not twiddle his thumbs waiting for a summons from Dr. Della.

Scanning the crowd, he finally saw her up ahead. The graceful way she moved, the cloud of soft brown hair that sat like a halo around her head. His pulse picked up speed and for a few dangerous seconds, he forgot why he needed to see her and simply appreciated her. But he wouldn't allow himself the indulgence for long. Too much was at stake.

"Nice day for a walk," he said when he drew alongside her.

As she turned, her eyes flared in surprise then narrowed. "Mr. Marlow. What a coincidence."

"Not so much," he said with a casual shrug. "The captain told me you had the day off."

"And you guessed that in a city of four and a half million I'd be in this exact spot." She arched a dark eyebrow. "Impressive."

A smile tugged at the corners of his mouth despite his best intentions. "The captain might also have mentioned that you have a fondness for the Gardens."

"Ah." She glanced across at a display of native flowers. "Considerate of him to throw that information around. Crew privacy is usually respected."

"I'm not a random passenger. And you're no longer a mere crew member of the *Cora Mae*."

"Perhaps, but I am still the ship's doctor."

Yes she was, but a young doctor with the world at her feet cloistering herself away on a ship made about as much sense as Patrick's will. He glanced over, looking for a clue, but he found nothing. He needed to understand—to work out what had happened with his uncle, it was important to figure out the woman who was at the center of it all.

"I've been wondering something," he said and dug his hands into his pockets.

Her eyes flicked to him then back to the trees they were passing. "I have a feeling I'll regret this, but tell me."

"I've seen your résumé. Why are you wasting your medical skills on a ship where you're hardly using them?"

"I see patients every day."

"For seasickness and sunburn?"

"Some of the issues are minor, but we're trained to handle outbreaks of contagious diseases and disasters out to sea. And passenger death is not unheard of. It's imperative that the ship's medical staff is highly trained and capable."

"I don't doubt it. But why would someone as young as you, with her whole promising career ahead of her, want to settle into a job where she could do ninety-nine percent of the tasks with her eyes closed?"

"I like the job," she said with a dismissive wave of her hand. "Is that what you tracked me down to ask?"

Cupping her elbow, he led her to the side of the path so he wouldn't have to share her attention with the plant life of Sydney. "We need to resolve the ownership of the *Cora Mae* sooner rather than later. I have a job to get back to—I'd only planned to sail this first leg to Sydney then fly back to Melbourne. I need an answer to my offer."

Her hand fluttered to circle her throat. "So soon?"

"Our situation has been reported on the news and if we leave it much longer, the uncertainty could affect my company's shares on the stock market."

"I don't know—" she began, but he cut her off.

"How about this? The ship is scheduled to leave Sydney at midnight. Come to my cabin for dinner tonight. We'll have privacy to thrash this out and come to an agreement. Then I'll disembark before the *Cora Mae* sets sail for New Zealand."

A tiny frown line appeared between her brows, then she blew out a breath. "You're right. How does five-thirty suit?"

"Perfect," he said and relaxed his shoulders. He'd resolve this and be on a flight to Melbourne in the morning.

They walked for a minute in silence, Luke's thoughts dwelling on Patrick and what he could have intended by leaving half the ship to Della Walsh, if he'd been thinking at all when he wrote the will. But the other thought that had been pestering at the edges of his mind was why Patrick had felt it necessary to keep his illness a secret from his own family. That's what family was for—to support each other in the hard times.

And if Patrick hadn't made the call, then his doctor should have.

He planted his hands low on his hips and found the gaze of the doctor in question. "I need to know something. Once you knew how serious Patrick's cancer was, once you knew he wouldn't survive it, why didn't you override his wishes and ring his family?"

Uncertainty flashed across her features. It had been fleeting, but he'd seen it. Then she found her calm composure again and crossed her arms under her breasts. "I have a question for you. Why didn't you ever visit Patrick?"

Regret and grief and guilt coalesced into a hard, hot lump in his gut. "That's irrelevant," he snapped. He didn't have to justify himself or his actions to a virtual stranger.

"Patrick invited you often." Her voice was soft, probing. "If you'd come aboard, especially in the last year or so, you would have found out for yourself that he was seriously ill."

"I've never been fond of sailing. Besides, I saw him when he came ashore so there was no reason." But that answer didn't satisfy the guilt that was eating at his gut, so he offered her a tight smile. "I need to get back to the ship to make some calls. I'll see you at five-thirty."

He turned on his heel and left.

At five-thirty, Luke showered and changed for dinner with Della. Walking down the stairs of his duplex suite, delicious anticipation sizzled through his bloodstream, making him pause. How long had it been since he'd looked forward to dinner with a woman this much? Della intrigued him—every word she'd said, every action, raised questions that begged him to find answers. Or challenged him the way she had this afternoon about Patrick. Either way, he was thinking about the lovely doctor far too often.

There was a danger in this.

He straightened his spine. He would not be distracted by a woman. His ownership of the *Cora Mae* was at stake.

He glanced around the suite's dining room. The concierge had offered him staff from the butler service for the night, but he'd declined. These negotiations were delicate and they'd need privacy.

He strode from the carpeted staircase to the living room bar and found it well stocked with spirits, wines and soft drinks. All contingencies covered. He knew little about Dr. Della other than that she lived on a ship and had medical training, but at least he'd be able to cater for whatever drinks she preferred.

As he was reaching for a bottle of white wine, there was a knock at the door. Bottle in hand, he crossed the room and drew the door open. His breath caught deep in his throat. She wore a simple floral summer dress and heeled sandals that accentuated her shapely calves. Her loose hair shone in the hall lights, and his hand twitched, wanting to reach out and wrap one curl around his fingers.

Della smiled, but her eyes remained wary, as if still considering the wisdom of this meeting.

He cleared his throat and opened the door farther to allow her to pass. "I'm glad you came."

"Thank you," she said softly, but didn't enter.

Placing a hand under her elbow, he gently guided her over the threshold. "Come in." When she took two small steps into the room, he closed the door and held up the bottle still in his hand. "Would you like red, white or champagne?"

She swallowed, her posture watchful and guarded. She was obviously deciding whether this meeting would be strictly business or whether she'd concede to a certain level of social nicety. He held her gaze, not pushing, not giving her the easy escape, either.

She nodded once, decision made. "White, please."

A spark of satisfaction zinged through his system—she was going to play nice. It would allow him more opportunity to resolve the situation just between themselves, without getting courts and lawyers involved.

He poured them both a glass of sauvignon blanc and showed her to an armchair. "Are you hungry?"

"I only had a light lunch, so yes, I am," she said.

He offered her the in-suite dining menu. "Since you're hungry, we should order now."

Della took the spiral-bound booklet but didn't open it. He realized she lived here—she probably knew the options by heart.

He leaned back on the couch and laid an arm along the top. "What would you suggest?"

"Depends what you like. Everything is delicious so you can't make a bad choice." She shrugged a shoulder then sat, still and watchful. He saw a way to create some trust that could move them past her guardedness and help the negotiations that would begin soon.

He closed his menu. "Why don't you order for both of us?"

Her eyes narrowed a fraction, assessing the sincerity of his suggestion. "How do you feel about Italian?"

"I could be tempted."

"Can I use your phone?"

"Please." He reached for the handset on the table behind the lounge and passed it to her.

She dialed, then lifted her gaze to him. "Hi, Angie, it's Della. Is Edoardo on tonight?" She smiled. "Can you ask him if he has enough of his eggplant parmigiana to send two servings up to Luke Marlow in the starboard owner's suite?" There was a pause. "Excellent," she said and disconnected.

He took the phone from her outstretched hand. "Am I right in assuming you've ordered us something that's not on the menu?"

"You would be right." She inclined her head, acknowledging his guess. "Edoardo used to occasionally make this dish for himself, then as people started tasting it, they'd put in a request for some the next night and it grew into a bit of a legend. Now he comes in early for his shift and makes a dish for any of the staff who want some. So he usually has a few plates' worth of it at the back of the kitchen."

There was a bigger story here—a piece of the Della Walsh puzzle. He gave her an unhurried appraisal. "You have three hundred and thirty staff members aboard the *Cora Mae*. He makes enough for them all?"

She shrugged. "Many work over the dinner shift, either in food service or entertainment, and on their break they eat at the staff canteen."

"There would still be a lot of staff off duty," he said.

As her lashes swept down then up, she reminded him of the movie stars of the sixties—beautiful, sophisticated and unattainable. One step removed from her surroundings, as if watching the world—him—from behind an impenetrable facade.

"Not all staff know about the secret parmigiana, do they?"

"We have a large amount of casual workers. They come on for a year to see the world, and then they leave to settle down somewhere."

"Not you." He took another sip of his wine and watched her over the rim.

"I live here," she said simply. "As do a core group of employees."

The people who'd formed the protective circle around Della after the will reading. The people who seemed to constantly stop to congratulate her on her windfall. "The parmigiana crowd."

"If you like."

He placed his empty glass on the coffee table and sat back. "Don't you think you'll want to leave to settle down on land at some point? Marry?"

"I won't marry," she said with certainty.

There was more to that, but he could see by the set of her chin she wouldn't share. Not that he blamed her for that attitude—his marriage to Jillian had been the worst mistake he'd ever made.

He changed tack, still trying to build some rapport so

she wouldn't be so resistant to him and would finally agree to sell her share of the ship. "Tell me about the *Cora Mae*."

Her eyes warmed. "She's a beautiful ship, a floating piece of heaven. A sanctuary." The last word was a murmur, as though it slipped out as an involuntary afterthought. She cleared her throat and continued. "The architecture of the shopping deck alone was a huge design task and won several awards."

Luke listened with half an ear as Della continued to espouse the merits of the ship, but one word replayed in his mind. *Sanctuary.* Why would Dr. Della Walsh—attractive, intelligent, well-educated—need a safe haven? She should have the world at her feet.

Perhaps it had something to do with that guarded expression he'd seen a few times, the one hiding an old hurt.

He caught himself, annoyed. What was he doing wondering about the private thoughts of this woman? That was a completely different matter to building rapport. He blew out a breath then met her gaze. Time to finish this charade.

"Dr. Walsh, what will it take for you to sell me all or part of your share of the ship?"

Four

Della cast a quick glance around Luke's suite—one small microcosm of the ship she loved, its gold-and-maroon furnishings, the rich wood and curved walls. What would it take for her to sell her share of Patrick's ship?

"It's not that simple," she said, shifting in her seat. "If I'd known Patrick was leaving me half the *Cora Mae,* naturally I would have told him not to. And in that conversation, he would have been able to explain why he was doing it. But I never had the chance to discuss it with him, so I'm not privy to his reasoning. And make no mistake, his reasoning faculties were sound till the end. How can I give it up if I don't know why I have it in the first place?"

Luke's shoulders tensed. This was obviously not the direction he wanted the conversation to be heading. "So, what—you're holding out for a secret letter, or a clue to his intentions?"

"Maybe. I don't know." Now that he'd said it aloud,

she realized she had been hoping a letter from Patrick would surface that explained his will, however unlikely that would be—if he'd written one, it would have been attached to his will, or in the papers the executor held. But there had to be *some* hint somewhere. "Surely we'll work out why he left it this way?"

"It's more likely that we'll never find out," Luke said, sounding as annoyed about that possibility as she was.

She crossed her ankles and smoothed her skirt over her knees. "I'm sorry, Luke. I can't give you an answer yet."

He rubbed his fingers across his forehead, as if he could smooth over the lines that had become embedded there. "Surely you don't *want* to be a part-owner?"

"Since coming to work and live on the *Cora Mae* two years ago when my father was captain, I've developed a certain sense of…ownership. I became good friends with Patrick, partly through his close relationship with my parents, and because of our frequent discussions about the ship, I often thought about changes I'd love to see."

"Your training is in medicine," he said slowly, "not in business management."

"That's a fair point. But I have lifelong observations of shipboard life. With my inside knowledge of how a ship works, having been part of discussions about ships with my family since I was a child, and later with Patrick, my input into the *Cora Mae*'s future could be worthwhile. And I have to admit—" she allowed a small smile to slip out "—part of me relishes the chance to try."

Luke tapped a finger on the table, his gaze not wavering from her face. "What about your medical career?"

"I always thought I wanted to follow in my mother's footsteps as a ship's doctor. But perhaps I'd like to follow closer to my father's path and have a greater say in this ship's future."

Eyes searching, he took a long sip of his wine and swallowed, as if biding his time.

"So now we've explored my intentions," she said, "how about you tell me what your plans would be for the ship. Would you keep the current Pacific route?"

He didn't move, yet something changed. Luke was suddenly a businessman again, looking at her with all the assurance of a CEO delivering a business plan. "There are still some details to be ironed out, but I'm planning to anchor her in the Great Barrier Reef as Marlow Corporation's first floating hotel."

"What? Why?" She blurted out the words before she could stop herself, her entire body recoiling from Luke's plan.

"Costs will be reduced by eliminating fuel and related expenses, and with the permanent location, guests would be able to get up close and personal with one of the seven wonders of the natural world. They'd have everyday access to excursions such as snorkeling the reef."

She sucked in her bottom lip. The idea of the *Cora Mae* no longer cruising the oceans as she was meant to was devastating. "Why not just buy or build a hotel on one of the islands? Tourism is already a booming industry up there."

"Land is limited," he said, unfazed by her dismay. "Most of the islands are already owned by tourism operators or are in private hands. Anchoring the ship will, in effect, create my own piece of real estate in one of the most desirable locations in the world."

"Wouldn't it have a dreadful environmental impact on the reef?"

He waved a hand. "Not at all. With the technology and systems we'd have in place for waste management, water and power generation, there would be virtually no impact at all."

"But, she'd be tethered to the one spot." Della frowned, not hiding her distaste. "Robbed of her freedom."

He smiled at that, then sobered. "It's a business decision. I can't let sentimentality trump financial factors."

"So, you'd chain the *Cora Mae* down to make more money. She'd have—"

She was interrupted by a knock at the door. Luke pushed out of his armchair and strode to the door, probably pleased by the distraction. A steward with an in-suite dining trolley greeted him, and Luke stood back to let him pass.

As the steward entered the room, she recognized him and smiled. "Hi, Max."

"Good evening, Dr. Walsh," the man replied with a flirtatious smile. Max had asked her out a couple of times in the past; she'd declined but he'd been cheerily optimistic about trying again in the future.

Luke looked sharply at Max, probably assessing the situation all too correctly. Then, as Luke's gaze landed on her, a warm shiver flittered across her skin. There was something in his eyes, a heat, a thought she couldn't quite read, but one she could tell involved her. The world around her faded as his silver-gray eyes held her spellbound. Then his jaw clenched and the connection vanished. He turned away and dismissed Max with the polite reply, "I'll take it from here, thanks," before wheeling the trolley to their table.

Della blinked, attempting to orient herself to the room again—the moment of connection they'd shared had been as intense as it had been brief and it had left her slightly breathless.

But it couldn't happen again. Forming an attachment to

any man—let alone the one she was in the midst of delicate negotiations with—was not in the cards. She folded
her arms tightly over her chest, reminding herself of the
scarred imperfection that lay beneath her blouse. The
mugger who'd stolen the life of her husband and left her
for dead had given her one last gift—a torso bearing the
scars of his stabs and slashes. A torso that would never
appeal to a man like Luke, who would be used to nothing
less than perfection.

She had no intention of baring those scars to anyone—
ever. Odd how her body seemed to have its own agenda,
not caring that it was so undesirable, only wanting a man's
touch, a man's caress. Luke's caress.

Involuntarily, her muscles tensed. For two years, she'd
lived a celibate life and preferred it that way. It was the
only path open to her—even in the unlikely event that a
man might see past her scars, she would never, *never* risk
loving and losing again.

"You know," she said with as much nonchalance she
could muster to cover her lapse, "that's part of Max's job.
To bring the food to the table and serve it." She stood and
moved across to the carved wood dining table, its glass
top set lavishly for a dinner for two.

Luke looked up. "I prefer that we're alone tonight,"
he said.

"So we can argue in private?" she asked, tensing.

"No, not argue, discuss." He gave her a crooked grin.
"Maybe it will be a little heated at times, but it's still a
discussion."

"Okay. A discussion."

"And while we eat, I propose a truce." He held her gaze
a moment too long.

She nodded once and took her seat, her false casualness evaporating. Something had changed between them. And she didn't have any idea how to undo it.

Luke served the two plates of eggplant parmigiana and refilled their glasses. Bending to place her glass before her emphasized the solid breadth of his shoulders, and she was struck by the disconcerting question of what it would feel like to touch the shape of the muscles that led from his neck to the tops of his arms. Shaking her head, she almost groaned—within seconds of wanting to undo the change that had happened between them, she was in danger of becoming carried away by a nice set of shoulders.

"Well, it smells good," he said, breaking into her thoughts.

She looked down at her plate. This dish had become her comfort food. She sliced a piece of the meltingly soft eggplant coated in crispy golden bread crumbs and popped it in her mouth, savoring the textures and flavor.

"How much of your childhood did you spend on ships?" Luke asked.

"From when I was three." She tucked a wayward curl behind her ear. "My father worked his way up to captain when he was quite young and with Mum being a ship's doctor, they raised me on ships across the world. I feel more at home on a ship than on land."

"What about your education?" he asked with a raised eyebrow.

"They homeschooled me, and after I finished high school, I went ashore and trained as a doctor."

He cut a piece of eggplant, but held it on his fork as he regarded her. "You said you came to the *Cora Mae* two years ago, yet your father was captain here for six years. Did you stay ashore after qualifying in medicine?"

She hesitated. Talking about that time in her life made everything inside her clench tight, but she took a deep breath and steadied herself to answer him. It was time to start moving through the stranglehold those memories had kept on her.

She looked down at her food, gathering herself, then up at Luke. "While I was training, I met someone. We married and set ourselves up on shore." How inadequate the words were to describe the love, the life that she'd shared with Shane.

"What happened?"

"He died," she said, her voice not even wavering, perhaps for the first time. "After, my father offered me a job and I took it. I might not have been aboard this particular ship before that for more than a holiday, but I…it felt like I was coming home." And that was more than enough said about her past. She took her last bite of eggplant and when she'd finished chewing, laid her cutlery on her plate.

They needed to get back on track. Back to focusing on their shared ownership of the *Cora Mae*. She fidgeted with her napkin. Perhaps it would be better if she came at it from another direction.

"How many hotels do you own?" she asked.

"Twenty-three, across Australia and New Zealand."

She might be responsible for people's health but it was one person at a time. She couldn't imagine the magnitude of making daily decisions for a company that large.

"Do you enjoy it?"

He stared at her for a moment as if he hadn't comprehended the question, then shrugged one shoulder and reached for his drink. "It's what I do."

A little window of insight opened before her and she couldn't resist peeking in. "But you must like working in the hotel industry?"

Luke toyed with the stem of his glass. "To an extent."

Della found herself leaning infinitesimally forward, intrigued. "Then why go into it?"

"It was my father's company, so I grew up working in it. From the kitchens and housekeeping when I was on school holidays, to the reception desk and the corporate headquarters when I was on university breaks." A rueful smile tugged at his mouth, as if he hadn't admitted this often. Or at all. "I don't really know any other industry."

It was sweet to hear of a father helping his son to get a leg up in the industry. "Was he teaching you at home, as well?" She could imagine his father talking about the business over the dinner table, explaining the decisions he'd made that day at work.

"I barely saw my parents," he said with a voice that was too neutral, too deliberately even. "I went to boarding school when I was thirteen. And, unless I was with Patrick, I worked in the hotels during holidays."

Della held her breath. Beneath his confident laid-back exterior, this man was covering a scar or two of his own. Patrick had never mentioned that Luke had been sent away to school, and now that seemed like a telling oversight.

"That must have been difficult. Lonely," she said gently.

He dismissed her words with a wave of his hand. "I think it's time we moved on to another topic."

He was right. It was none of her business how he was raised. She took another long sip of her wine, then brought the conversation back to where it needed to be. "Were you serious about turning the *Cora Mae* into a floating hotel?"

"One hundred percent. I've looked into it in the past, so my staff has already done some of the background work and created a plan. Right now they're hard at work hammering out the details."

A sudden thought struck—was this the real reason Patrick had left her half the ship—he'd known what Luke intended and wanted Della to prevent it?

She laced her fingers together and took a breath. "Had you talked about this plan for the *Cora Mae* with Patrick?"

He blew out a dismissive breath. "I'd broached the subject."

"And?"

Luke shrugged. "He could see the merits of a permanently anchored cruise ship as a hotel."

"But what about the *Cora Mae?* Did you discuss her specifically with him?"

"Not in any depth. There was no need to. This was several years ago now and Patrick was still fit and healthy with no hint of the cancer that was going to kill him."

"I see." She dabbed the edges of her mouth with the napkin, then laid it carefully on the table. "There's no doubt in my mind that Patrick would have wanted the ship to keep cruising. I think this is why he left me half the *Cora Mae*—so that I could stand as her advocate after he'd gone."

Luke speared his fingers through his hair. "Much as I wish Patrick was still with us, he's not," he said, his voice a little rough around the edges. "We can't run a business trying to second-guess what he wanted. We have to do the best we can at the present time."

How simple that sounded. How convenient and neat. But it wasn't the way she worked. She moistened her lips and lifted her chin a fraction. "I'll do everything in my power as a half-share owner to keep the *Cora Mae* cruising." It was her responsibility. She wouldn't let Patrick down.

"Della, you can't afford to buy me out, so your vision for the ship will be hard to implement. We'll either need to agree, which is seemingly unlikely at this point, or you need to sell me a portion of your share."

"But why does it need to change? The ship is profitable, isn't it? You can appoint a manager. You can appoint me. I'll carry on the work that Patrick did. There's no reason for the *Cora Mae* to be tied down and her engines left to rot."

"Except profit, Della. It will be much more profitable if she is tied down."

"She's special, Luke. If only you could look past the size of the black numbers on the accountant's balance sheet, you'd see."

"Profit is the bottom line," he said patiently. "That's the way the business world works."

"And the way you work."

"To me, it's second nature." Something in his expression flared to life as he spoke the words.

She lifted her wineglass and sipped as she considered him. She needed to understand him to have any chance of changing his mind. "It's more than that, isn't it?"

He nodded, conceding her point. "It's life itself. My business is the only thing in my life that's never let me down. The only constant and reliable aspect. People, on the other hand, shift their loyalties with a change in the wind. They can never be relied on in the tough times." His gaze suddenly snapped back to hers as if only now realizing how much he'd revealed. Deep frown lines appeared across his forehead.

"I'm sorry," she said. It wasn't her place to pry. "I shouldn't have—"

He shook his head, dismissing her concern. "If nothing else, I think we've established that we're coming from two completely different places, so we'll have to agree to disagree on certain aspects of our situation."

He was right, of course, but there had to be another way. There was always another way.

"Tell me, what do you think of the ship so far?"

"She seems nice enough," he said as he refilled their wineglasses.

"She is. You could live here full-time and never miss the land."

His gaze sharpened. "You never miss the land?"

"Never. But I meant the guests," she said before he could use her comment to focus back on her. "We have all the services you could possibly need, from hairdressers to a day spa to fine restaurants." She ticked off amenities on her fingers as she went. "You're already familiar with the business resources, the internet and cell phone access. And for recreation, the rock climbing wall, tennis courts and ice rink are hard to beat. There's even half an acre of lawn on Deck Twelve if you miss the feel of land beneath your feet or want an on board picnic."

Luke arched an eyebrow. "So you never yearn for a city or a town?"

"There are more facilities here per person than in a city, and every few days we stop at one of the world's most exotic locations." And that was the key. Sailing from port to port was the essence of cruising. Of the *Cora Mae*.

Luke put his knife and fork on his empty plate and pushed it to the side. "I can see the appeal, Della. But I won't base a business decision on the idea that sailing is a charming lifestyle."

Della rubbed a finger against her temple where the pressure was building from her mind whirling. Sailing was about more than charm—she had to find a way to show him. It seemed there was only one option left.

"Luke, I have a request. Give me one month aboard the *Cora Mae* to convince you of the merits of cruising, of changing ports regularly. Before you make any other decisions about its future or we make any agreement about ownership, give the ship a real chance."

He drummed his fingers on the table and she wondered if she'd asked too much. A month for a businessman in Luke's position was a long time, even with the resources the *Cora Mae* had at his disposal for keeping in touch with his office.

Then he steepled his fingers. "I'll give you three weeks, but while I'm being open about the idea of a cruising ship, you need to be sincerely considering selling me a portion of your half-share, regardless of whether the ship is permanently anchored in the future or not."

"I can do that," she said, relieved. Convincing him in three weeks wouldn't be easy, but this was a challenge she couldn't back away from.

Luke raised his glass to make a toast and when she lifted hers, he clinked them together.

"Let the persuasions begin," he said with a smile.

Della floated in the crystalline blue water off a secluded beach in New Zealand's Bay of Islands. Days ashore weren't always something she took advantage of given that each location came around every four weeks, but the Bay of Islands was one place she always sneaked out to when she could. Cal Bateman was on call today, so Della was gloriously free.

Well, except for her Luke Marlow mission.

She glanced over at her mission a few body lengths away, swimming farther out in long, easy strokes, then back again. Did that man ever relax? Even when he was still, he was like a tightly coiled ball of energy.

He surfaced near her and wiped a hand across his face. His hair was much darker when it was wet, and slicked back it accentuated his gray eyes. Made them hard to look away from. Here, insulated from the real world by the blue, blue water and the powder-white crescent of beach, she could almost believe they were just two people spending time together because they enjoyed each other's company. Where she could swim the short distance separating them and wrap her arms around his broad, bare chest.

He moved through the water with the ease of a seal, and when he surfaced again, closer this time, his bare torso was slick with water. Her fingers wanted to reach out. But that would be to fall into the delusion that they were just two people out for the day, together because they wanted to be.

Instead, she was here to sell him on the concept of South Pacific cruising.

"You really take those sun safe messages you give the passengers to heart, don't you?" Luke said, indicating the long-sleeved Lycra shirt over her swimsuit.

She shrugged. "I'm afraid it's the result of having very fair skin, combined with knowing too many medical facts about the skin cancer rates in Australia and New Zealand." With the added advantage of making absolutely sure none of her scars peeked out.

"Among the highest rates in the world," he said, drifting closer. "I saw the information in the passenger briefing notes. In fact, I paid attention and applied a generous layer of sunscreen, Dr. Walsh."

"Very good," she said, trying to sound professional. Because she'd noticed. And despite making herself look away from his hand rubbing over his chest and shoulders as he stood on the sand, she'd still managed to watch from the corner of her eye.

"This place is great," he said, taking in the scenery that

surrounded them. "I've been to New Zealand more times than I can remember but never this spot."

"I'm guessing you usually fly over for meetings?"

"And there aren't too many of them on the beach," he said, acknowledging her point. "Though, much as I'm enjoying myself, why exactly are we here?"

She arched an eyebrow. At 7:00 a.m. she'd left him a message to meet her in the lobby and bring his swim trunks, and he'd been there, ready and waiting. She'd assumed the reason for their excursion had been self-evident.

"You've forgotten our agreement already?" she said sweetly. "Too much sun, Mr. Marlow?"

"The agreement was about the *Cora Mae*. Unless you're on the payroll for New Zealand tourism on the side?"

"Cruising is about so much more than the ship. It's also about the locations you can access, like this place." She swept her arm in an arc. "You spend a day or two in the luxury of the ship, then you arrive at another exotic destination. That's something a floating hotel can't offer."

"Fair point," he said, but she couldn't tell if he was humoring her or not. "So, what's in that basket I carried here?"

"Picnic lunch courtesy of the restaurant." The lunch baskets were one of the ship's specialties and passengers were invariably impressed with the quality of food as well as the small touches.

"I was hoping you'd say that. Is eleven too early for lunch?"

She smiled widely. "The beauty of life on a cruise is it's never too early or late for anything. The day is ours to order how we want. It's a step further removed from the everyday than a vacation at a hotel."

"Well, we wouldn't want to waste the opportunity." He grabbed her hand and pulled her toward the shore. His fingers were strong and warm and they sent a spray of champagne fizz through her blood, from her fingertips, to her arms and out to every cell in her body. There was no stopping it, so she dived under the water, using the action as an excuse to break the skin contact with Luke, then slicked back her hair when she emerged.

As she walked up the white sand to the shade where they'd left their things, she kept a respectable distance from the man walking beside her. This was not the time nor the man to allow herself to indulge in flights of fancy over. Especially when she had no idea if the charm he was displaying today was genuine or if it was part of his not-so-subtle plan of convincing her to sell her 50 percent. Tricky man, Luke Marlow. One not to underestimate.

She pulled the Lycra sun-shirt off over her head, and rubbed herself down with the large beach towel. As she grabbed her T-shirt she saw Luke's gaze land on her collarbone. She glanced down and saw the shoulder straps of her conservative swimsuit had moved enough to show the edges of her scars. Hands moving quickly, panic flaring in her belly, she adjusted the straps and pulled the T-shirt over her head.

Luke watched Della and frowned. The way she tracked his eyes and shied away told him something was wrong and for some reason, he wasn't prepared to let it go. She'd pulled the T-shirt on to cover any trace of the marks that marred her skin, but he stepped closer and gently pulled the neckline to one side to expose them. To prove to himself they hadn't been his imagination.

"Della, what happened?" he whispered.

"It was nothing." She turned but he moved with her, his fingers still brushing her collarbone.

"Scars like that don't come from nothing."

She didn't move. Not a single muscle. "I meant nothing important."

"It looks important. Della, won't you tell me?"

She winced. "You could find out how I got them with a simple internet search. It was in all the papers at the time."

A sense of foreboding filled the air, surrounded him, almost choked him. He cleared his throat. "I don't want to read impersonal newspaper articles. I want you to tell me."

She looked out to sea, her face too pale, her features pinched tight. "It was two years ago. There was a woman," she said, her voice unsteady. "Walking through Melbourne late at night, my husband and I heard her screams. Shane was a doctor, too, so we went to see if we could help."

Luke picked up her hand and gently stroked the creamy skin from her knuckles to her wrist. "Of course you would."

"She was down a laneway, where it was dark and deserted." She paused. Swallowed hard. "Alone except for the four men who surrounded her."

His heart thudded hard against his ribs, as if ready to physically leap to her defense. But he was several years too late, so he stood silently instead.

"We couldn't leave her," she said urgently, finding his gaze.

Squeezing her hands, he held her eyes. "I wouldn't have been able to leave her, either."

She nodded. "Shane started down the laneway, calling out, hoping to distract them. I pulled out my mobile phone and rang the police. Before I could give my location, one of them grabbed the phone from me and smashed it on the wall. They'd left the girl and were heading for us."

"Oh, Della," he said on a long breath. His whole body was too tense, wanting to stave off what had already happened.

"When I looked past the men, the woman was gone, which was the good news." She smiled, but it was the saddest expression he'd ever seen.

His eyes flicked to the scar peeking out from under the collar of her T-shirt. "The bad news being that now there were four men focused on you and Shane."

She was silent for a long time, and Luke waited. His fingers stroked the back of her hand, his other hand rubbing up and down her back. Inside he was burning with anger, with the injustice of it. But Della didn't need his anger. She needed strength, comfort and support, so he stuffed it all down as well as he could and kept rubbing her back.

"I woke up in the hospital. Thankfully, the woman had run for help. They were too late for Shane. He'd been stabbed in the chest multiple times, and the blade had pierced his heart."

Her hand felt cold, so he reached for her other one, too, and held them between his, as if he could will heat and strength into them. "I'm sorry."

Tears slipped over her cheeks and she looked out to sea.

"What did they do to you?"

"The same. Left me for dead, but they weren't as thorough and the surgeons repaired the damage."

There was nothing he could say, so he pulled her close and held her against his chest, hoping that he could soothe the tiny tremors, and that, as she relived the memory, she at least felt safe in the present moment. What had he been thinking? He was ten kinds of stupid for making her tell him the story.

Part of him wanted to distract her so she didn't have those images in her head. Kissing her senseless was the option of choice—she wouldn't be able to think of anything else, and it would satisfy the clawing need inside him. But that would be taking advantage of her at her most vulnerable. So instead, he continued to hold her.

One thing finally made sense—her aloofness with men, whether it was the flirtatious steward who'd delivered their dinner or, not least of all, Luke himself. The reason she'd pulled away when he'd noticed her scars had been embarrassment, possibly even shame. Della Walsh was unsure of her desirability. He could tell her how ridiculous that was, how she affected *him,* but she wouldn't believe him. And it was definitely the wrong time to show her. No matter that his pulse had spiked the moment he'd felt her soft curves against him as he held her and that it had yet to settle.

Finally she stirred and pulled away.

"I'm sorry," she said as she swiped at her face.

"No, Della, I'm sorry. I shouldn't have asked. You should have told me to go to hell."

One corner of her mouth twitched and his chest expanded with satisfaction that he could relieve her darkness even a little. "In fact, you can tell me to go to hell now."

Her lashes lifted as she looked up, checking to see if he was serious. "I'm supposed to be on a mission to convince you of the merits of cruising. So I don't think I'll be saying that."

But there was a spark returning to her features, and her face wasn't as pale.

"To be honest," he said, running with the idea, "you'd be doing me a favor. If we leave it like this, I'll be weighed down with more guilt than I'll know what to do with. At first it will affect my mood, but eventually it'll affect my interactions with people and my work. I could lose my friends. My company could go bankrupt."

"Is that right?" she asked, amusement beginning to dance in her eyes again.

"It would be devastating. The only way I can see to avoid total destruction is if you retrospectively pull me into line."

She ran a hand over her damp hair. "I don't—"

"Make sure you use my name when you do it. I'd be very grateful."

She chuckled and, after her desolation minutes before, it was a sound sweeter than any he could imagine.

"Go on," he urged and nudged her shoulder with his. "You know you want to."

She broke into a proper laugh and held up a hand. "Okay. Just give me a moment." Her expression turned somber but her eyes still danced. "Go to hell, Luke."

"That was good, but I didn't believe you. Try again."

Her mouth fell open in amused outrage then she took a deep breath and narrowed her eyes. "Go to hell, Luke."

There had been more heat in her words this time, but as soon as she finished, it all fell away and she bit down on a smile, as if surprised at her own daring. "Better," he said softly.

"You should be careful," she said with an arched eyebrow, "or that might become my new favorite phrase."

He'd thought he wanted to kiss her before. Now the need to draw her close and capture those lips was as strong as any need he'd felt. To fit her along his body and feel her curves against his skin. The air was suddenly too thick to breathe; he couldn't fill his lungs. Her eyes darkened and the pulse at the base of her throat fluttered. She felt it, too. There wasn't a thing in his life he wouldn't give to be able to lean in, to touch that mouth.

He wouldn't. She was still vulnerable from retelling that story and he would never be a man who took advantage of that.

He scrubbed a hand down his face and looked out to sea.

But it wouldn't be long.

Sometime soon, he'd find the right time and place to kiss Della Walsh.

Five

The next morning, Della met Luke for a tour of the ship—one of her "persuasions" to convince him to keep the *Cora Mae* in her current state. She'd racked her brain for little bits of information, any anecdotes that Patrick had told her about Luke that she could use now. She had a lot of material to work with, from an ex-wife who Patrick had hated, to Luke's impressive grades at university. But nothing that would work for her in this situation.

Then she'd recalled the perfect detail. A cook in one of the galleys had worked on one of Patrick's ships when Luke was a child and, when Della had checked with her, the cook remembered him. It was the ideal place to start. If they could get Luke to make an emotional connection to the *Cora Mae,* he might let his heart contribute to his decision.

He was so focused on cold, dry factors such as profits and spreadsheets, that before she could convince him not to permanently anchor the *Cora Mae,* they needed to be at least talking the same language. A combination of head and heart. To do that, she had to engage his emotions in the debate. Only then would she have a chance to change his mind.

Hands low on his hips, looking more devastatingly gorgeous than any man had a right to be, Luke regarded her as she arrived. "Where's our first stop on your magical mystery tour?"

"We're starting at the beginning. Belowdecks, in Galley Two."

"And here I'd expected another day of leisurely swimming."

She remembered his bare chest glistening with water droplets yesterday, and board shorts sitting firmly over a taut abdomen. Then she remembered how her body had reacted when he'd simply taken her hand in the water, and her blood began to heat.

She swallowed and turned her gaze ahead. "Maybe some other time."

But not until she'd recovered from the memories of their first swim, at a minimum.

"So is there a dress code for these tours?" he asked, rocking back on his heels.

She cast a sweeping glance over his casual trousers and polo shirt. "What you're wearing won't be a problem for today."

"Do you say such sweet things to all the boys, or is it just me?" he asked, gray eyes twinkling.

"Fishing for a compliment, Mr. Marlow?"

"You know what?" he said and cocked his head to the side. "I'm perversely enjoying the novelty of not receiving them."

Chuckling, she shook her head. "Dear me, what a tough

life you must lead to be jaded by a steady diet of compliments."

"Praise, sincerely given, isn't a bad thing. When it's simpering or calculated, and part of an agenda, it's tiresome."

With his wealth, power and those sculpted cheekbones, she could imagine he received regular insincere compliments. She reached out and pushed open the double-hinged doors to the galley. "Then I'll make a concerted effort to keep all simpering to a minimum."

"Your generosity knows no bounds," he said dryly and walked through the open door.

She threaded her way through the counters and staff until she found her quarry. "Hi, Roxie."

A middle-aged woman with round, rosy cheeks and faded red hair held high on her head in a bun turned and smiled widely. "Dr. Walsh. So lovely to see you." She took Della's hand in both of hers then leaned to look past her. "And this must be Mr. Marlow all grown up. I'd heard you were on board, but I didn't think I'd get to see you again."

A faint line of concentration appeared between Luke's brows as he offered Roxie his hand. "Have we met?"

"I don't expect that you'd remember, but when you were a little boy, you'd sometimes come down to the galley of the old *Princess Cora* and visit me."

Della crossed her fingers behind her back. Before she could make more headway with Luke, she needed something to sneak under his defenses. Hopefully Roxie would do it.

Suddenly, the frown line disappeared and his eyes widened. "Mrs. Appleby?"

Roxie beamed. "One and the same."

"You used to sneak me sultana cookies," Luke said, his eyes alive with memories.

"They were your favorite." Her face dropped. "I'm so sorry about your uncle. He was a good man."

"Thank you. I appreciate you saying so," he said, his features carefully schooled to neutral. He glanced around, then turned back to Roxie and lowered his voice conspiratorially. "I don't suppose you still bake those cookies?"

Roxie grinned. "They haven't been on the menu lately, but I baked a batch yesterday when I heard you were on board." She lowered her lashes and a little extra color rose in her cheeks. "Just in case."

"I haven't had a good sultana cookie since I was twelve." Luke smiled the charming smile that probably got him whatever he wanted. "Don't suppose that new batch is nearby?"

"Let me get a paper bag."

As Roxie bustled away, Della bit down on a smile. She hadn't won—not by any stretch of the imagination—but they'd just taken an important step in getting Luke to think of the *Cora Mae* as more than spreadsheets and figures, and she was well satisfied with that for now. She introduced Luke to one of the chefs who was still working on late breakfasts and they chatted about the kitchen's capacity and appliances. When Roxie returned with a brown paper bag neatly folded over at the top, Luke turned the charm back on. "I appreciate this, Mrs. Appleby."

"You just let me know when you want more. I'll bake a new batch whenever you need."

Della said goodbye to Roxie and led Luke out through the swinging doors.

"I'll treat you to a cookie," he said, holding the bag aloft. "There has to be at least eight in here."

"Only if I can buy you a coffee to go with it." She had to keep moving ahead—not lose the momentum Roxie had given her.

"Deal," he said.

She took him to her favorite café, A Taste of Paris, on the shopping deck, where the French chef made pastries that melted in the mouth and coffee that tasted like heaven. She snagged a table on a paved area outside the café's glass shopfront, a spot that would allow them to watch passengers splurge in the stores along the main shopping strip.

"I'll go in and order," she said. "How do you like your coffee?"

"Black, double strength."

When she came back a few minutes later with the coffees and two empty plates, she found Luke sitting with his back to the glass wall, his long legs stretched out in front of him, watching the world go by…the world of shipboard retail, at least. He opened the paper bag and offered it to her. "You knew about Roxie Appleby sneaking me cookies when I was a kid."

"Patrick told me." In fact, Patrick had delighted in regaling her with stories of Luke's school holiday escapades.

Luke laughed, a gorgeous full-throated sound. "Here's me thinking I'd been a juvenile master of espionage and indulging in some serious rule-breaking and the old devil knew all along."

She just smiled. She wasn't going to tell him that Patrick had been pleased to see his too-serious nephew getting up to mischief.

He took a sultana cookie from the bag and dropped it on his plate. "And you took me there deliberately, to attempt to establish an emotional connection between me and the staff."

She smiled angelically. "I wouldn't be giving it my best shot if I'd let the opportunity slip by."

"It's reassuring that I'm not in the hands of an amateur," he said and bit into his cookie.

"I also wanted you to put faces to the people who are depending on us. The people our decision will affect." The same faces that haunted Della's mind when she thought about the choice that lay before her.

He sipped his coffee and watched her over the rim. "But Roxie would keep her job if the *Cora Mae* becomes a floating hotel," he said as he set the cup back in its saucer. "Nothing need change there."

"Roxie might not want that job. She spent a few years on land after you knew her and had a family, and now she has a son working here on the bridge, a daughter in Sydney and another son in New Zealand with his wife and baby. I suspect she'd look for another ship doing a similar run if you anchor this one, so she could still see her children regularly."

He frowned as he finished his cookie and brushed the crumbs from his fingers. "You're not suggesting I should direct the future of my company based on where Roxie Appleby would prefer to work."

"No, of course not. I'm just helping you get to know the ship and her crew and the issues they face." Baby steps. And this baby step was merely to raise a niggle of doubt in his mind about how perfect his plan was. Which led to the next baby step. "I'm on duty after lunch but we still have some time before that. We could go ice skating, try some golf, play a game of tennis—the whole ship is our oyster. Or, how do you feel about rock climbing?"

He shrugged one shoulder. "I prefer golf."

"Mini golf, driving range or the putting green?" She ticked off the options on her fingers.

He rubbed his jaw, considering. "Depends."

"I'll tell you up front that I draw the line at being your caddy."

The edges of his sensual lips twitched. "Nice to see

you're willing to go the extra mile for your cause. But fortunately, you don't need a caddy for any of those options."

"Then what does it depend on?" she asked warily. In the short time she'd known him, she'd learned to expect the unexpected with Luke Marlow.

"Do you play?"

"I've played mini golf. What about you?"

"Never played a round of mini golf in my life," he said, obviously holding back a wince. "But real golf—" his eyes flared with passion "—that's a game I've indulged in."

Della smiled brightly. This was good news. She wanted him relaxed, enjoying himself—in the best possible mood while considering the *Cora Mae*'s future. "How about we try the driving range?"

"Sure, why not?" he said and stood.

She looked up at him, so tall and broad as he loomed over her, and her heart skipped a beat. Suddenly she could think of several reasons why not, chief among them that watching his powerful shoulders as he took a swing would likely mess with her focus on making her case for the *Cora Mae*.

She drew in a breath, pushed back her chair and stood next to him. She'd just have to be extra vigilant. Besides, she didn't *have* to watch him. She'd take a few swings herself—the activity might help her to keep her mind somewhere else.

Luke watched Della line up another shot in the driving range's nets. The golf pro on duty had tracked their shots on the computer software and given them some statistics such as the ball's speed and trajectory, plus a few tips for improvement. Then he'd moved on to another passenger in one of the three nets and left them alone to practice.

The power in Luke's shots wasn't as good as usual, but

he tried to ignore the twinge in his palm from the stitches and play on regardless.

Della put her feet together beside the tee, then moved them shoulder-width apart as Luke had shown her when they'd arrived. Her back was straight, her knees a little bent, and her sweet rear end was angled slightly, ever-so-enticingly out. She drew the club back, then a loud thwack split the air and, with considerable effort, Luke dragged his gaze away to watch where the ball hit on the net's target.

"You sliced again," he said as if he'd been watching the whole shot, not dividing his time between that and her rear end. "But not as badly."

"Do you say such sweet things to all the gals, or is it just me?" she said, recycling his words from earlier.

"What can I say? You bring out the best in me."

"Smooth talker." She pulled a face at him before bending to put another ball on the tee. "This is harder than mini golf."

He barely managed to hold back the laugh. "Just a bit," he conceded. "Though you're a natural. If I didn't trust you, I mightn't have believed this is your first time."

As the words left his mouth, Luke stiffened. *Trust her?* When had he come to trust her? His gut clenched tight. Looking back, something had changed yesterday at the Bay of Islands. Hearing her distress while telling him her story, something inside him had shifted.

Trust gave her all sorts of power over his business future…maybe even over him. He wasn't sure he liked that. In fact, he was damned sure he didn't.

And if he trusted her, then he could no longer believe she coerced Patrick to leave her half the ship. Although Patrick meaning to leave her half the ship made no sense at all.

Della moved back to let him have a turn and he stood in front of the tee, gripped the club as well as he could with the stitches in his palm, moving his arms, feet and knees to slip into the correct posture. Then he remembered where his eyes had been while she'd taken her shot....

Where were her eyes now? Would straitlaced Dr. Della do something as naughty as watch his butt while he swung? His pulse leaped but he took a breath and focused on the ball. Banter was one thing, and he might believe her story about Patrick now, but he wouldn't let himself become entangled with someone he was in business negotiations with. No matter how her rear end looked when she swung a golf club.

He lined up the shot, drew back the club and hit the ball with a satisfying thwack. He put another ball on the tee and stood back for her turn.

"What time do you go on duty?" he asked.

"Midday," she said without looking up. "Are you attempting to distract me?"

No, he thought, *to distract myself.* "Can't blame a man for trying."

"I'm just learning this game and already you're being competitive?"

He waited till she took the shot—another slice, but again, not too bad all things considered—before replying. "Competition is hardwired into my brain. Comes with having a Y chromosome."

She wrapped her fingers around the handle of her driving iron, her eyes calculating. "How about we make a wager then?"

"On hitting into the nets?"

"Too hard to score. On mini golf." She flicked a glance at her watch. "The clinic closes at three, so plenty of time for a play-off afterward."

He'd never seen the course and he'd guess she'd played it many times. Her familiarity with the holes versus his putting skill might just produce an even contest. "What are the stakes?"

"You win, we continue with the current plan of persuading each other about the *Cora Mae*'s future. I win, you leave the *Cora Mae* as a cruising ship."

He didn't try to hold back the laugh this time. "Nice try, Dr. Walsh. Lucky for me folly wasn't wired in with my competitive spirit. Let's make the stakes more in keeping with the game being played, shall we? If you win, I'll go rock climbing."

"Not challenging enough," she said, tapping one slender finger on her club's shaft. "I win, you spend a day at the ship's day spa."

He winced. "Will that involve fluffy white towels and green slime plastered over my face?"

Her lips twitched. "So I've heard."

"You've never been?" he asked, intrigued.

She shrugged, seemingly unfazed by his question. "I've been told by trustworthy people that the services are first-rate."

"Okay," he said slowly. "You win, I'll go to the day spa. I win, you go."

Her eyes rounded. He'd surprised her. A potent coil of satisfaction twisted tight in his belly. "Deal?" he prompted.

"Deal," she said.

He lined up the shot and swung, knowing he was far too pleased with himself over merely surprising Dr. Della.

At half past three, Della took the elevator to the top deck and strolled over to the mini-golf course. She'd changed into shorts and a white sleeveless wraparound top, running shoes and a baseball cap. She was here to win. Getting Luke to agree to some time being pampered had been on her agenda, but she'd known it would be a hard sell. If she won this match, problem solved. Luke would spend time at the day spa, relaxing, building positive memories of the ship to reinforce the rest of her strategy. She wanted him head over heels in love with the *Cora Mae,* so he'd want what was best for the ship, not his bottom line.

She saw him ahead, leaning casually against the counter, silver-rimmed sunglasses covering his eyes, feet crossed at the ankles, the recipient of adoring looks from the girl running the activity desk.

Della took a moment to appreciate his long lean form before Luke lifted his sunglasses to the top of his head as she approached. She glimpsed heat flare in his eyes for a split second before he smothered it. "Della, I was just telling Christina about our wager."

Christina's blond ponytail bobbed as she nodded. "I think it sounds like heaps of fun. Good luck," she gushed, eyes never leaving Luke.

Della smiled wryly. Luke had an admirer. Though, she had to admit, if she—who'd sworn off men—was affected by Luke's magnetic aura, then a less seasoned woman like Christina didn't have much hope.

They took their clubs and a scorecard and moved off to the start line, with more of Christina's good luck wishes following them.

"Apparently, you have your own personal cheer squad," she said as she wrote their names at the top of the scorecard.

"She's a nice kid," he said, and a little part of her—one she wasn't proud of—warmed at his easy rebuff of the attentions from a pretty girl. She chanced a glance at him again to check, but his eyes were roaming the first hole. It was fairly straightforward—a green felt S, relatively flat.

"I'd normally flip a coin to see who goes first," he said, "but I think ladies should go before gentlemen."

"I suggested the match, which makes you my guest, so you go first."

He arched an eyebrow. "Looks like we'll need to flip, after all." He dug into his pocket and drew out a shiny silver twenty-five cent coin. "Heads or tails?"

"Tails."

With a flick of his thumb, the coin spun into the air, turning over and over, catching the sun on each rotation. Then he plucked it out of the air, planted it on the back of his hand and held it out for her to see. Heads.

He stuffed the coin back in his pocket and rested the club across the ledge of his shoulders, behind his neck, with a wrist holding it in place at each end. "I'm ready to be dazzled by nine holes of your mini-golf brilliance."

"Right. So no pressure, then." She dropped the ball onto the black X and lined up the shot. If she could bounce it off the first curve at the right angle, it should end up somewhere near the hole. She surveyed the angle of the S and found the spot on the little white barrier wall she'd need to hit.

"You strike me as a person who thrives on pressure," he said, but she ignored him as she aimed for the spot she'd found and swung. The ball touched close to where she'd aimed, bounced away and struck the side again farther down, then rolled along to within a couple of feet from the cup. A fairly straightforward putt.

Only then did she look up at him. "Trying to distract me again, Mr. Marlow?"

"It's a pretty high-stakes game, Dr. Walsh. Nice shot, by the way."

She walked the S then hit the ball into the hole before stepping over the ankle-high wall so Luke could take his shot. He hit the spot she'd been aiming for, but it still didn't give him a hole in one. Just left him a little closer to the cup than she'd been. He tapped it in and strolled over. "We appear to be even."

"It's only been one hole," she pointed out as she recorded his score on the card.

The next hole, the windmill, put him one stroke ahead. They were back to even after the third, a hilly U.

"You don't play like a man who's never been on a mini-golf course before."

"What can I say? It's a ball game, I'm a man."

"A match made in heaven," she teased and sneaked a glance at him. No doubt that he had an athlete's body—strong shoulders, muscled chest tapering to narrow hips, biceps and forearms that flexed as he lined up his club—but even so, mini golf was its own basket of skills.

"Yep." He grinned. "You know, I feel obliged to point out that this course would be just as accessible to guests if the *Cora Mae* were permanently anchored."

"Ah, but it's more about doing something fun on the deck of a moving vessel—the exhilaration of feeling the ship sail through the water while you're playing sports is something that can't be replicated on a floating hotel."

Luke glanced at the ocean, rubbing his chin as he considered. "I'll take your word for it." He took his shot, then looked back up at her. "Have you played the course often?"

"Occasionally, when there aren't many passengers wanting to play. It's a shame it's such a clear, calm day. My specialty is playing when the going is rough." In truth, even then the ship barely rocked at all, but it was enough to affect a shot.

"A stroke of luck for me," he said with a lazy smile.

Though she was starting to wonder if it was simple luck, or if Luke's entire life was charmed—even the weather cooperated.

With six holes down, Luke was ahead by two strokes. "When you go to the day spa," he asked with an innocent air, "will you have a manicure, as well? Or a pedicure? I like the idea of your toenails in a red gloss polish."

She waited until he was about to swing. "Got a foot fetish?"

He laughed and hit badly, the ball bouncing from a little wall of cobbled rock almost back to where it had started.

"Oh, what a shame."

"Mmm." He glanced down at her sandals. "Definitely red…or perhaps a flaming scarlet."

"You're only two strokes ahead, Mr. Marlow," she said moving to set up her ball. "Try not to get carried away."

After she won that hole, she was only behind by one. She picked up another stroke on the eighth by again using his trick and distracting him before he hit, leaving them tied going into the last hole. Della bit down on her lip as she recorded the scores. If she could just get Luke to consent to all the delights of a day spa—warm oil massage, hot rocks, sauna—he might relax enough to be in a better frame of mind for her to sway him to keep the *Cora Mae* a cruising ship. All she had to do was to get him there, and to do that she needed to win this game. With the score even, it came down to the ninth hole. She squared her shoulders and laid her ball on the black cross.

Luke watched Della place her ball and size up the path to the cup. She wanted to win, that much was obvious, but he'd planned how the game would end before either of them had taken their first swing. He might not have played mini golf before, but he knew one end of a putter from the other, and he'd played more games of billiards than he'd had homemade dinners. Same principles to both games—it was all about angles and momentum.

Making the game's outcome seem natural, that was the tricky part.

Luckily he'd won the coin toss and would play the ninth after Della. It was a complex path that led over a steep slope, under a footbridge, around a fountain and to the cup. In many ways it reminded him of his relationship with Della herself—overly complicated and too many distractions preventing him from keeping his eyes on the prize.

Della managed it in four strokes. Luke thought he could do it in three. Four if he made a mistake—an actual mistake, or a deliberate one. He glanced up at Della and murmured, "Wish me luck."

"Sure," she said sweetly. "Here's to you winning a day at the spa."

"I appreciate the support," he said, then took his first shot. It passed over the hill, under the overpass to hit the side of the fountain before rolling to a stop. He was on track to win the hole. Win the round. Which was not on the agenda.

Della wanted him to spend a day at the spa, and he was willing to do it. He'd been serious about keeping an open mind regarding the *Cora Mae,* and was willing to go along with all the plans Della had to convince him to keep her cruising. Just as he hoped she was doing the same about the ship's transformation into a floating hotel.

But if he had to be trapped in the den of sweet smelling horror that he'd heard passed for day spas, then it was only fair that she had to go, too. Plus, he was curious that she lived here and hadn't paid a visit to the place where women were pampered. His eyes skimmed her delectable form. Unless… Perhaps this was about the scar he'd seen while they were swimming? She'd been so quick to cover it up and stop him from seeing any more of it—did Della have body image issues? He frowned as he walked around the outside of the ninth hole to reach his ball.

"Awkward spot," she said.

"Not too bad." As he lined up the shot, his skin warmed and he knew Della had moved closer. She was going to try and distract him. And he was going to let her. How long had it been since this doctor had spent any time being spoiled? Indulging herself? Too long, he suspected. Time to rectify that. He restrained the smile that threatened.

He swung the putter back and, on the downswing, Della said, "How are your stitches?"

He botched the shot and the ball ended up a little farther behind where he'd started. "Your concern for my health is touching," he drawled, eyeing his ball with a mocking expression. "And useful."

"Surely, you don't think I tried to put you off, Mr. Marlow. Why, that would be despicable. No—" she assumed an angelic expression "—I'm simply honoring my commitment to a patient and to the Hippocratic Oath."

He took a step back and lined up his next shot.

"So your hand isn't bothering you with the grip on the club?" she asked, moving around into his field of vision.

"It's a little tender, but nothing to worry about. I'm doing most of the work with my other hand." It wasn't like he had to put any force into these swings, so this was easier than hitting in the nets earlier. He made the shot and thankfully it hit the place he was aiming for, making it around the fountain on the rebound.

He couldn't win. But he could tie.

His last shot got the ball in the cup. "What's the score, doc?"

"We tied," she said, frowning. Clearly this outcome wasn't a welcome turn of events.

He grinned. "So, I guess we'll both be off to the spa."

Perhaps the grin was a step too far. Hand on hip, she scrutinized him with narrowed eyes. "Why do I get the feeling you planned it this way?"

He rested the club behind his neck, along his shoulders. "You have a suspicious mind?" he said helpfully.

"You said you hadn't played mini golf before."

"I haven't, but I play a lot of billiards. The principles are the same."

Shaking her head, she flashed him a resigned smile. "I've been scammed."

"Maybe, but if the day spa is as good as you say, then we're both winners."

She laughed, and as she did, her nose crinkled up. His heart stilled in his chest and the rest of the world seemed to recede. Dark hair danced around her face in the light breeze, and there was humor in her bottomless brown eyes. Nothing short of the world ending could have stopped him from laughing with her. Until he realized what he'd done.

He'd started to relax.

For the first time in far too long, he felt like he was actually taking a holiday. Despite the grief of losing the uncle he'd loved, and the mountains of work he'd managed while Della had been on shift. Despite his deep-seated aversion to relaxing around anyone but his billiards buddies because it inherently involved letting down his guard.

Despite knowing Della was someone he was locked in a high-stakes business negotiation with, someone who tugged at him so much, he knew he needed to be extra careful around her. And possibly most seriously, despite vowing that he'd never again be blinded by a woman to the detriment of all else. He silently cursed himself.

Tension flowed into his muscles, bracing his shoulders, then pouring through the rest of his body, tightening and clenching until he felt...more like his normal self. That was a disturbing thought. He filed it away for later consideration. He took down the club from his shoulders—a stupid, cocky pose—and rested it on the ground, the grip of his good hand tightening till he felt his knuckles straining.

Right now he had other, more important matters to concentrate on. He set his jaw and met Della's eyes again, this time being sure to keep his expression more suited to a business acquaintance. "So what's on the agenda tonight?"

Her eyebrows quirked, obviously noticing the change in his demeanor. The happy twinkle vanished from her eyes and he knew it was in response to his suddenly chilly tone. It made him realize just how much she'd relaxed with him.

She took a small step back and nodded with a respectful detachment. Perversely, he already missed the secret delight of the casual air that had sprung up between them. And didn't *that* just show how important it was that he'd caught his slip in time?

"I think you deserve a night off," she said with that damned polite smile she'd used when he first met her.

A reprieve. Time to get his mind in order. Just what he needed. So why did he want to push?

"Why waste the night?" he said before he could stop himself.

She bit down on her lip, then her shoulders squared. "I have some paperwork to do this afternoon, so I'll be grabbing something quick for dinner. But I can see you after that. Meet me at the main staircase in the foyer at seven."

He nodded. Before then he would get his head thinking clearly again. Because, starting tonight, they were changing tack—he was going to convince Della Walsh to allow him to turn the *Cora Mae* into a floating hotel. No more messing around.

This was business.

Six

While Della waited at the stairs for Luke that evening, she fingered the scalloped neck of her top. It was new, more daring than anything she'd worn for the past few years. The moment she'd seen the gleaming sequined mint-green garment in one of the ship's boutiques, she'd had to have it. Given her refusal to wear anything but relatively plain clothing since her husband's death, she'd found her obsession with the top disquieting. Could it be a sign that she was changing? She glanced at the fabric with the tiny gleaming discs, habit making her check that her scars were well covered.

She looked up to see Luke strolling into the lobby and all thoughts flew out of her mind. The same magnetic charge that had struck her the moment she'd first seen him on the deck hit her again—it held her gaze steady on him, enticing her to draw closer. She ran her palms down her skirt and tried to hold on to her composure. His hair was damp and freshly combed; his sky-blue dress shirt emphasized the breadth of his shoulders and chest. A need to feel that strength under her hands was so strong it threatened to pull her under.

"Good evening, Della," he said, granting her a lazy smile. "You look amazing."

"Hello, Luke," she said brightly, hoping to cover how her pulse thrummed. "Thank you. Is there anything in particular you'd like to do tonight? See one of the live shows, perhaps? Try the wine bar?"

He sank his hands into his pockets. "I assume this ship has a dance floor?"

"There are three venues," she said, relieved to be able to fall into tour guide mode. "If you like a modern atmosphere, there's a nightclub on Deck Five. And there's a retro disco on Deck Nine. Or if you prefer a waltz, the Blue Moon is on Deck Four."

"Which one do you usually go to?" He raised a lazy eyebrow.

Butterflies leaped to life in her belly. She had a feeling she knew where this was going—the wrong direction.

"I—" she began but her throat was too tight to speak. She swallowed and began again. "I don't." Even to her the answer sounded sharp, full of meaning. Not just a statement of fact as she'd intended. When he raised his eyebrows, she found herself compelled to say more. "I'm not much of a dancer. But I'll take you to whichever venue appeals. I'm sure you won't have a problem finding partners."

"I'd rather dance with you," he said, his voice as rich and smooth as darkest chocolate. Before she could think of another excuse, he held out his hand. "Live on the edge. Dance with me, Della."

She looked at the hand outstretched in front of her.

This wasn't just a hand she'd sutured; it was a man's hand. She hadn't held—*really held*—a man's hand since her husband's. It was loaded with meaning. An invitation to dance. Her mind spun on to the next threat...dancing, which required even more body contact than handholding. Involuntarily, her muscles tensed.

For two years, she'd lived a celibate life and preferred it that way. It was the only path open to her—even in the unlikely event that a man might see past her scars, she would never, *never* risk loving and losing again. So why go dancing? Or even share dinner with a man?

Because Luke wanted to—and she'd locked herself into a game of "persuasions" to convince him to keep the *Cora Mae* as a cruising ship. A game she didn't intend to lose. So no backing away from a simple request.

Though, if she were honest, part of her wanted to dance with this man. Would it be so wrong to give in to that part just this once?

Ignoring the trembling deep inside, she took Luke's hand and showed him the way to the Blue Moon.

As Luke led her onto the full dance floor ten minutes later with a firm grip on her hand, Della tried to remember how to breathe. She normally loved that the walls around them were painted darkest blue and studded with fairy lights that resembled little stars, but for the first time she couldn't spare them a glance.

He's walking you to a dance floor, not off a gangplank. No big deal.

But her body wasn't listening. Because, any moment now, Luke would take her in his arms—a touch more intimate than any contact from a man she'd experienced in several years. Her stomach tightened like a fist.

While the singer crooned an old favorite and with other couples scattered around them enjoying the night, they reached the center of the polished floor. Luke turned to face her, inviting her to step in. She tried to comply—to move—but her feet wouldn't work.

You agreed to this. You said you'd dance with him.

Taking a breath, she shuffled her feet until she was encircled by Luke's patiently waiting arms. Perhaps sensing her inner tension, he held her at a respectable distance and began to move them smoothly around the floor. She was as stiff as a board, but was helpless to loosen up. Being this close seemed wrong on so many levels.

"I won't bite," he said, his mouth near her ear.

Startled from her thoughts, she caught her bottom lip between her teeth. Of course he wouldn't; she was being unreasonable. They were simply dancing, the same as the other couples. The same as she used to do. Before.

Consciously loosening her muscles, she released some tension as she exhaled in a long steady stream.

"Better," he murmured.

His encouraging tone allowed her to relax more into his arms. And as she did, she became aware of the sensation of those arms around her—supportive and…nice.

The scent of a man's clean skin filled her head, and the strength of his broad shoulders registered under hand. Her pulse picked up pace, and this time it wasn't due to apprehension. He pulled her almost imperceptibly closer, and she looked up into his warm gray eyes.

"I'm sorry," she said, not knowing exactly what to say.

"What for?" he asked, his voice soft. "You've given me an entertaining day and now you're dancing with me. There's nothing to apologize for. I should be thanking you."

Kindness with no awkward questions. Her heart melted a little. The depth of his sensitivity was unexpected. She couldn't have picked a better partner for her first foray into dating. Not that this was a date, but the things they were doing were all the sorts of things normal couples did when they went out. Maybe, after Luke left, she would make more of an effort with her social life, stop cutting herself off—not go searching for a relationship, just a little company. Maybe it was time.

She smiled up at him. Other guests floated across the floor, most dressed to the nines, several dripping in diamonds or brightly colored gemstones, but she ignored them. They couldn't compare to this man.

He shifted his hand at the small of her back and rubbed a slow pattern of small circles, sending goose bumps rushing across her arms and torso. As he led her in a turn, he pulled her a little closer again. A space still existed between their bodies, but she could feel the heat emanating from him, and his breath fanning over her cheek.

Suddenly she didn't want his kindness, didn't want his gentleness. She wanted to be dragged against him—closer still—to feel his body pressed against the length of hers, to kiss and be kissed. It had been so long...

The strength drained from her body, leaving her cold. *How could she be thinking such things?* Wanting to kiss a man who wasn't her husband? Wanting to start something that could only lead to another ending either sooner or later.

She stumbled to a stop, thoughts clashing in her mind, the rigidity returning to every part of her body. How easy it was to counsel others on the stages of grief, on the turmoil of the road to recovery. The importance of not being crippled by guilt when normal needs and desires start stirring again.

She looked up at Luke. "Would you mind—?"

"Can I get you a drink?" he smoothly interjected.

"Thank you," she said, more grateful for his under-standing than the drink. "A lime and soda."

He guided her over to two vacant bar stools and ordered her drink plus a scotch. Then he turned and casually surveyed the room. Perhaps to give her more time to recover.

"Looking for anyone in particular?" she asked.

"Not really." He turned back to her, all relaxed charm. "I've run into a few acquaintances in the corridors and around the ship, but you're the only person on board that I actually know."

His words unsettled her. "You don't know me, Luke," she said softly. There were so many things about her that he didn't understand.

"I think I do." His gaze rested on her mouth. "Or at least I'm coming to."

She moistened her suddenly dry lips. "Are you also coming to know the *Cora Mae?*"

He looked from the pianist sitting at the baby grand to the twenty-foot-high wine rack behind the bar and nod-ded. "I believe I am."

Their drinks arrived and she flashed a smile of thanks to Tommy, the bartender. She took a sip, then put her glass down on the polished wood bar. "Dare I hope she's grow-ing on you?"

"I've become very fond of her," he said, but she couldn't tell if he really meant it, or whether he was humoring her.

Swirling the ice around her glass, she asked, "Can you see that she deserves to stay cruising the South Pacific?"

"I see your point, Della, I do," he said, spearing his fingers through his hair. "But this has to be a business decision, not a sentimental one."

She laid a hand on his forearm. "Surely it wouldn't be charity if it makes a profit."

"I don't know anything about running a cruise ship."

He placed a hand over hers as it lay on his forearm. "If I take the time to learn, it will divert my time and energy away from my own business, so I need to be very sure."

Her chest tightened and she withdrew her hand. She'd thought it was a simple matter of convincing him about the merits of cruising, but she now saw the mountain she'd need to overcome before he'd agree to leave the *Cora Mae* alone.

He took a sip from his drink and swallowed. "Tell me more about yourself, Della."

"There are so many more interesting topics." She resisted the impulse to squirm in her seat.

"You said I didn't know you. I'd like to."

"But it's not necessary, is it? Not part of the business we're involved in here. Time is precious and I need you to know about the *Cora Mae* and her crew." She ran her finger around the rim of her glass. "Did you know we have a three-story auditorium with live shows?"

Slowly, deliberately, he sat back on his stool and regarded her. Della held her breath. He was deciding whether to pursue the topic or let her off the hook—it was in the look he leveled at her. And she had a feeling that if this man pushed hard enough, she might just tell him anything he wanted to know.

"All right," he said finally, lifting his glass. "Tell me about the crew."

She breathed a sigh of relief. For whatever reason, he was allowing her to change the subject. "Well, there's the medical team, of course. Then there's our social activities team," she continued. "They organize the program of events such as the games and yoga in the mornings."

"Do you join in the organized activities?"

She practiced yoga on her own during quiet times at the gym, not in the group sessions. Having her scars peek out of her leotard during a pose and catching people's attention was not her idea of relaxation or recreation. "I'm not much of a joiner."

His slow blink told her she hadn't fooled him. "You never miss the land, yet even out here you're not much of a joiner. Interesting."

Her chest tightened. "Stop trying to decode me, Luke," she said and picked up her drink.

Luke could see he was losing her again. She'd begun to relax when they were dancing, then something had made her pull away. Despite knowing it was a bad idea, part of him wanted her back there, wanted her in his arms again. Having her there had felt damn good. Better than anything had in too long to remember. He held back an oath. Time to leave the dance club.

"I've only caught glimpses of the top decks so far," he said. "Will you show me?"

She nodded, relief sliding over her features. "Of course."

He settled his hand at the small of her back as they wove their way through the throng, and had to restrain a sigh at how good even that small touch felt. The thin fabric slid smoothly over her skin and he had the illusion that at any moment he could pull her close and wrap her in his arms—closer than she'd been when they'd danced. Close enough to feel her pressed against him. He curled the fingers of his free hand into a fist then stretched them. How would he keep his reaction to her under control for three weeks?

The clear glass doors of the elevator opened and they stepped in. As they began the ascent, he glanced at the passing levels…until he realized Della was watching his reflection. His breath caught. When his gaze met hers in the glass, she didn't look away. The effect of the stolen glance was electric, and his shirt collar was suddenly restrictive around his throat.

After an eternity encapsulated in mere moments, the elevator slowed and the doors whooshed apart, taking the reflected image of the two of them with it, and the tension that had been building in his chest dissipated.

"This is the second highest deck," Della said as they stepped out. The oddly intimate connection was gone and she was all business as she pointed up, to their left. "That's Deck Thirteen, the highest, but it only has a bar and a cluster of heated spas."

He looked up and saw people spilling out the doors of the bar, the beat of rock music floating down to where he stood. Their deck—Twelve—had only two other people, a couple strolling much farther along, absorbed in each other. "It seems fairly empty."

"It usually is at this time of night. Most people are at dinner, or the night entertainments like the theatre, or they're at a bar."

"Or dancing," he murmured, remembering the feel of her in his arms.

"Or dancing," she agreed neutrally, seeming not to be as affected as he was by the memory. "During the day, this is a popular area, though. This pool is always full of guests, and the deck chairs are used by people reading or relaxing."

They walked past a long, curved pool, with underwater lights that made the water sparkle. Before their picnic at the Bay of Islands, he couldn't remember the last time he'd been for a swim. It must have been years—leisure activities weren't high on his priority list. He worked out at the gym in his office building, sure, but that wasn't for fun, that was to keep himself healthy. He paused and looked down into the glittering depths; depths that were unexpectedly enticing. "With these facilities, you must have a dip in the water every day."

"I don't swim here," she said smoothly.

He turned to her and sank his hands deep into his pockets. "You swam with me in New Zealand."

"Usually I prefer privacy." She moved away and pointed to their left. "Have you seen the life-size chessboard?"

And it clicked into place. Her scars. She was self-conscious about her body. He wanted to take her by the shoulders and tell her she shouldn't worry—a few scars couldn't ruin her beauty. But he knew that would fall on deaf ears. He stared at her a moment longer before turning to the chessboard and her question. "I can't say that I have."

She ran a hand over the smooth top of a white pawn that came up to her shoulder. "Can you play?"

"Sure. Can you?"

"I haven't in years—" she hesitated and her eyes flicked to him and back to the board "—but I'll give it a go if you'd like a game."

Luke arched an eyebrow. This was a diversionary tactic. Della obviously wanted them occupied in an activity that didn't involve touching. Sensible woman. Logically, he should be striving for the same thing. No, not should. Would. He *would* be aiming for such activities.

"I'll take black," he said, moving to the opposite side of the board.

Della stepped across the squares and pushed one of her pawns two squares forward.

"Predictable start," he said as he picked up his knight and placed it on a square in front of his line of pawns.

She moved another pawn out. "Just because something is predictable doesn't make it wrong."

"Perhaps." Lifting the pawn diagonally to the right of his bishop, he moved it out one square. While she thought about her move he watched her, but he saw her sneak a self-conscious look at him from under her lashes. His scrutiny made her uncomfortable. She was a mass of contradictions—she surveyed the world with calm composure, rarely missing a thing he was sure, yet didn't want to be observed herself.

And whenever he asked her a question about herself, she gave brief replies, but talking about the ship or her crew, you couldn't switch her off. It wasn't modesty holding her back in discussions about herself—sharing personal information made her uncomfortable. Why would that be? Was it connected to the personal history she'd shared that day on the beach?

He looked up to the stars and a flash of movement caught his attention. Within an instant he was beside Della, one arm around her waist, pointing skyward. "Shooting star."

"Oh," she said on a long breath, her gaze following his finger.

The feel of her against him was mesmerizing. Absorbed in the moment, she'd forgotten to be on her guard and allowed her soft curves to meld into his side, her head resting back on his shoulder as she tracked the star's path.

"Make a wish," he murmured beside her ear.

A kiss. In this moment, all he wanted was to turn her to face him, to lean down and touch her sweet lips with his. It was wrong, he knew it was wrong, but the blood in his veins thundered and a delicious heat began to rise.

The star faded and the night sky again grew still, the only movement the ship's steady forward progress and the gentle breeze that danced in Della's hair. But she didn't move away. Part of him dared not move and break the spell, but the larger, rebellious part of him—surrounded by the scent of vanilla and woman—risked inclining his head down to hers, and was rewarded when she shivered.

"Like to know what I wished for?" he said, voice low.

Her eyes drifted shut. "You're not supposed to tell. It won't come true if you do."

"Maybe," he said, his mouth so close to her ear that his lips brushed her lobe as he spoke. "But if you knew what the wish was, perhaps you'd grant it."

He pressed a light kiss on her neck, just below her ear. Della held herself still but didn't pull away. "I don't have any magical powers to grant wishes."

"I'm not so sure." He pressed another kiss to her soft skin, this one at the edge of her jaw.

As he cupped the side of her throat with one hand, he felt her racing pulse and turned her to face him. A small sound of protest passed her lips even as she leaned in and placed the lightest of kisses on his mouth. It took everything inside him, but he locked his muscles tight and didn't move an inch. Della had held herself back so much, he wouldn't ruin this by pushing too far, too fast. Instead, he waited for excruciating seconds for her to come back to him. Her warm breath caressed his face as she looked from his mouth to his eyes, fighting some inner struggle. Then she tilted her head forward and stole another butterfly kiss, and again, he gently moved his lips but nothing else, despite the protests of his straining body.

Her scent curled around his thoughts, leaving little reason in its wake, but he held firm until she tipped her chin up for a third time. Now, her lips were more confident and she wound her arms up around his neck. That was all the permission he needed, all the permission he could wait for. With a groan, he pulled her in.

He deepened the kiss, tasting her, needing to be close,

connected to her. Holding her flush against him with the hand she'd stitched, he traced a path over the curve of her spine with the other, down over her hip, back up to feel the swell of the side of her breast. He'd wanted her from the moment she'd first appeared like an angel from the crowd on the deck the day he'd boarded, but now, he craved her with an urgency that rocked him. His body was ablaze; the kiss was nowhere near enough. Her fingers wound up into his hair and dug into his scalp, her mouth demanding against his.

"Della," he rasped as he wrenched his mouth away to drag some oxygen into his lungs.

She stilled and looked up at him with eyes that were suddenly alert...and stunned.

"It's okay," he whispered as he rubbed a thumb over her damp bottom lip.

She unwound her arms from his neck and let them fall to her sides. "No, it's not." She said the words quietly, almost to herself, her eyes averted. Then she drew in a deep breath and met his gaze. "Luke, you don't want to do this."

He almost laughed at how far that was from the truth. "I can tell you that my body disagrees in the most strenuous of terms."

"That's because it's under a misapprehension."

"What would that be?" he murmured as he skimmed his fingers down her spine to the dip in her lower back, trying to bring the two of them back to the place they'd been only moments earlier.

For a full second, her eyes darkened in response to his caress, before she blinked the effect away. "Your body thinks there's a chance this will go further."

"Hate to be the one to break it to you," he said lazily, "but your body agrees with mine."

She pressed lips still rosy from his kiss tightly together. "Luke, you have to know something."

"I'm listening," he said, watching the way her mouth moved, wanting to lean in again and—

"No, you really need to hear this."

His gaze flicked up to her eyes. She was right. He was paying more attention to her mouth than the words coming out of it. Summoning all his self-discipline, he took a small step back and rested his hands on his hips. "Okay, shoot."

"I'm celibate." There was a pause as he thought he'd misheard or she'd been joking, all while she watched him warily.

"Celibate?" he finally said, frowning. "Are you serious?"

She nodded as she folded her arms under her breasts. "I don't want to lead you on, to waste your time."

His mind grappled with the concept, which seemed so alien to his hormone-drenched body. "You took some kind of vow after your husband died?"

Della drew in a breath and moved the short distance to the guardrail. He followed and rested his forearms on the top rail, facing slightly away from her to give her some space.

But she apparently didn't need it—she turned to him. "No vow, but this is not a flippant lifestyle choice. I'm serious." A soft pink flush touched her cheekbones—this was difficult for her to share. Which just made it harder to understand.

"You don't kiss like a celibate person," he murmured.

"I'm sorry about the kiss. That was a mistake," she said, her gaze not wavering.

Something deep in his chest protested. "Not from where I'm standing."

"It was the first time I've kissed anyone in two years.

It won't happen again." Her voice was filled with quiet certainty. When he opened his mouth to reply, she held up a hand, palm out. "There's nothing you can say or do to change my mind. Please don't make this awkward by trying."

He let out a long breath then gently tucked a wayward curl behind her ear. "Even though I'd love you to change your mind, I do respect that you've made your decision." He rubbed an index finger across his forehead. "I'm asking questions because I'm intrigued." Everything new he learned about this woman intrigued him.

"Is this about your scars? Do you doubt I desire you?"

She shook her head slowly. "It's more complicated than that, but please don't ask me more. You're the first person I've told, and I'm only doing it now to stop you wasting any more time pursuing an impossibility." A smile pulled at the corners of her mouth, but it was unconvincing. "I've tried to head this off a few times but you're persistent."

He returned the smile, acknowledging the truth in that. "I appreciate your honesty. I'm more disappointed than you know, but it's your decision to make," he said, still not understanding, but willing to leave it for now.

"Thank you," she whispered.

After he'd walked her back to her room and left her without so much as a kiss on the cheek, Luke went back to the deck and leaned on the same railing they'd shared minutes before. Dragging in a deep breath of ocean-fresh air, he looked up at the stars again. He sure hadn't seen that coming. How could a woman who kissed as passionately as Della be celibate?

And, though he was serious that he would never push her to breaking a decision like that, he was more keen than ever to understand what made her tick.

Seven

Della froze at her desk as the nurse's voice floated from the front room through her partially open door.

"Good morning, Mr. Marlow," Jody said. "How can I help you?"

Hidden in her office, Della bit down on her lip and wondered if she could shut the door without drawing attention. She'd successfully avoided Luke Marlow since their bone-melting kiss. For a full day yesterday. Despite knowing she only had a short time to convince him about the *Cora Mae*.

She sighed. Her procrastination had to end now.

"I'd like to see Dr. Walsh about the stitches in my hand," he said, voice deep and charming.

Even from this distance, the timbre of his voice seemed to reverberate through her body, and her eyes drifted closed. Memories of their kiss surfaced in her mind—the way his hand had curled around the nape of her neck, the champagne fizz that had rushed through her veins the moment his lips had touched hers.

"I'll just see if she's available," Jody said out in reception.

Della's hands fluttered to the desktop and clasped together. Two years ago, she'd lain in a hospital bed critically ill with the injuries she'd received in the attack that had killed her husband. Shane had been her everything. Having his life ripped from her in that dirty street had been unbearable, overwhelming. In her grief, she'd made a promise to herself—never, never again would she love someone enough to leave her vulnerable to that much pain.

Intellectually, she knew she couldn't, *shouldn't,* hold herself to that long-ago promise. But emotionally, she knew it still held sway over her. Exposing herself meant stripping bare in so much more than just a physical sense. And Luke would be horrified if he ever caught a glimpse of the puckered scars across her torso. He might think he knew about a couple of dainty marks, but the reality was uglier. Anything physical between them would end before it had begun.

Not that it would ever get that far. All she was doing now was stopping things prior to reaching that point. Saving him the trouble. Saving herself the pain.

Jody slipped in through the doorway and closed it behind her. "Do you want me to pass him to Cal?" she asked quietly.

As strong as the temptation was, she knew she couldn't. She'd asked Jody and the other staff in the medical suite to cover for her if Luke rang. She hadn't explained why, and they'd been considerate enough to not ask questions. She simply needed time to get her bearings—to purge that kiss from her memory so she could focus on the reason for seeing him.

So she could face him merely as a business associate, the other half-owner of Patrick's ship. Calm, professional, unperturbed.

That meant no passing him to Cal now.

"That's fine, Jody." She drew in a fortifying breath. "Show him in."

All too soon, Luke sauntered into her office, one hand deep in a pocket, the bandaged hand held at chest height, his dark blond hair rumpled, as if he'd been on the top deck in the breeze. She remained behind her small desk, grateful for the illusion of protection it afforded her.

"Jody tells me your hand needs attention?" she said, starting the conversation as she meant it to continue—on a professional basis.

The arch of his eyebrow showed he'd noted her tone, but he didn't comment on it. Instead, he glanced down at his bandaged hand. "I think you might need to check this."

"Certainly," she said, smiling. "Jody? Can you come in here a moment?"

The nurse appeared at the door. "Yes, Dr. Walsh?"

"Mr. Marlow has some concerns about his sutured hand. Can you take down the dressing and check for signs of infection while I bring up his report, please?"

Jody nodded, holding back a smile as she washed her hands in the sink. Surprise flared in Luke's eyes, then an almost imperceptible frown as he no doubt calculated strategies to circumvent the proceedings, followed by amusement as his gaze flicked to hers and he realized he'd been outmaneuvered.

She sat back down behind the desk, feeling unreasonably smug at gaining the upper hand.

Jody moved to the table where Della had first sewn the sutures. "Mr. Marlow, if you'll take a seat and lay your hand here, I'll take a look."

In her peripheral vision, Della saw Luke set his hand out on the flat surface. After pulling up his info on the computer screen, she swiveled in her chair to find his eyes on her as Jody peeled back the bandage. As the wound was exposed, it looked exactly as Della had expected— a healthy pink with the skin healing around the sutures.

Jody wiped the area with an alcohol-infused cloth. "There's no sign of redness or swelling. Have you had any pain?"

Still looking at Della, he said, "It doesn't hurt, but I couldn't say things have felt right."

Della's stomach lurched as she took his double meaning, and she threw a quick glance at Jody, but thankfully the nurse didn't seem to notice anything amiss.

Jody pressed Luke's hand gently with her gloved fingers. "Any pain when I do this?"

"No."

Della glanced at the screen to check the date. "The stitches have been in for long enough, anyway. Jody, you can take them out."

While the nurse efficiently removed the sutures, Della made a few notes in Luke's file. With Luke watching her, the skin at the back of her neck tingled the whole time. A shiver ran up her spine, but she refused to look around.

When Jody finished, she stood, stripped off her gloves and looked to Della. "Do you need me for anything else?"

"No. Thank you, Jody," Della said, and watched the nurse leave. Then her eyes strayed to the man who remained.

"If that's all—" Della said at the same time Luke said, "You didn't return my call."

She took one breath, then another. "I haven't had a chance yet."

"You were avoiding me," he said softly, taking a small

step forward. "You told me where you stand and I said I respected that. Why would that stop us from spending time together?"

Something inside her trembled, knowing this was a make-or-break point. And she had to be completely honest. She moistened her lips.

"You don't expect more?"

"I wouldn't be averse to something more. But I think you already know that."

"There's no future with me, Luke."

"I can accept that. I'm not after a future but I do want to explore what we do have here and now," he said.

She wrapped a hand around the taut muscles at the back of her neck. He wouldn't be interested in something short-term either if he knew what she looked like under these clothes. A shipboard fling was all about fantasy, about glorious experiences. Her body allowed for neither.

"Besides," he said, moving to the side of her desk, "you were convincing me of the merits of keeping the ship sailing the high seas. Surely you haven't given up on that?"

"No," she said slowly.

"It's much harder to convince me from the other side of the ship."

"I—" she paused and swallowed "—I just thought we both needed a bit of a time-out."

"But we're past that now?" He stroked his fingers across his chin and her skin tingled as if he'd touched her own chin.

She drew in an uneven breath. "Perhaps."

He nodded once, short and assured, as if she'd agreed with him. "I've been thinking about what you said last night."

"I thought you might. But we—"

"It's about your scars, isn't it? Your celibacy is because you don't think you're desirable."

She flinched. It was one thing to think about it, another to have her insecurities presented so boldly to her face. But she couldn't lie. "Partly."

She didn't elaborate—she wasn't ready to talk about the pain of loving and losing with Luke Marlow, or anyone for that matter.

He stepped closer. "It must be hard to contemplate baring yourself for the first time after what you suffered. Hard to trust that you won't be rejected."

"Yes." Her throat felt thick and tight. His understanding was her undoing.

"You can trust me, Della," he said, his voice low as he took another step closer.

"You think that but you don't know…you don't know." She swallowed.

"Della—"

"Anyway, it's a moot point."

He looked at her with such genuine concern, she felt a tiny chink in her resolve.

"What if I guaranteed my cabin would be in total darkness?" He reached out and cupped the side of her face in his palm. "Would your answer change if you had that privacy?"

Her eyes drifted closed as she instinctively nestled her face into the warmth of his hand. He really did understand. There was a thrill in knowing he wanted her enough to create a way she could feel safe while being intimate. Intimate. Making love with Luke Marlow…

She was sorely tempted.

Her heart skipped a beat. Shane had been her only lover and she'd made vows before God that he'd be the only one. But her husband was gone forever. The scars on her body had insulated her from facing this decision…but now there was Luke. Could she take what he was offering?

She swallowed. "I honestly don't know."

"I'm having dinner in my cabin tonight." His gray eyes sparked with invitation. "Join me."

"And if I say no to your offer to turn the lights off?"

"Whatever your decision, you're welcome to share dinner. I'd prefer your answer was yes," he said with a smile in his voice, "but I'll respect a no. We still have much to discuss with the *Cora Mae,* regardless."

Join him. Such a simple request.

And maybe things between them *should* be that simple….

Maybe she was making this into something bigger than it needed to be. They'd kissed. She'd told him they had no future. He'd accepted it. Time to move on. Back to the plan.

"I'll let you know."

"While you're deciding, think on this." He moved in close, crowding her, and then his mouth came slowly down until it softly, firmly moved over hers. A molten heat flared at her core, filling her body cell by cell and she moaned. The push of his tongue, the brush of his arms at her waist, his scent surrounding her…she was lost.

Just when she was trembling with need, he slowed the kiss and eased away.

"All right, then," she whispered.

She watched a slow, satisfied smile spread across his face as he turned and walked through the door. And her stomach fluttered as she realized she may have miscalculated her ability to handle Luke Marlow.

Della knocked on Luke's cabin door that night, no closer to a decision about taking their attraction to the next level than she had been in the medical suite.

Once taken, that step would be impossible to undo. And if he reacted badly to her body—if he was horrified, or pitied her—would she be able to continue to negotiate with him about the *Cora Mae*...or would she burn with an unhealthy mix of embarrassment, hurt and resentment making business discussions impossible?

There was no way of knowing how any of the variables would play out.

At her first knock, the door swung open and he stood before her in a black polo shirt and tan pants, stealing her breath. His gray eyes were dark, his chin freshly shaved and he filled the doorway as if it were a frame made just for him.

For a charged moment, neither of them moved or spoke. The air was heavy with the possibilities of the night, sending a shiver through her blood.

Then he reached out and drew her in, placing a chaste kiss on her cheek. "I'm glad you came."

"Did you think I wouldn't?" she asked, her voice only a little unsteady. The merest contact of his lips with the side of her face sent magic shimmering across her skin, and she wanted to turn to him. Ask for more. But she wouldn't let herself get carried away—she'd need a cool head to make a decision tonight that was right for her.

As she passed him, he cupped her elbow. "I hoped you would, but I've learned not to assume anything with you."

She glanced around the room, taking in the soft lighting, the flickering candles, the two glasses sitting on the table. The stage was set for seduction. She swallowed. As for what may happen tonight, she was trying hard not to think about it just yet.

Luke indicated the bottle of white wine in the ice bucket. "How about you pour while I organize dinner?

Roxie Appleby sent me up a basket with instructions that are apparently foolproof."

"Sure," she said, grateful for something to do with her hands. She normally wasn't prone to restlessness, but standing close to Luke Marlow, close enough to smell his cologne, while they were surrounded by candles and low lighting, created an…unsettled feeling deep inside.

An unsettled feeling? Is that the best you can do to describe it after all those years of medical training? Della laughed softly at herself as she poured the wine. Her amusement dissipated her tension just a little until she took the glasses to the kitchenette, where Luke was tossing a salad. The action drew her gaze to the solid breadth of his shoulders, and she wanted nothing more in that moment than to smooth her hands across them. She'd bet they were solid. And warm. And smooth. Her pulse raced erratically. If she said yes to his proposition, she could run her hands over those shoulders tonight. Impossibly, her heart beat faster.

"Would you like yours in here?" she asked through a dry throat.

"Here's great." He laid the utensils down and took the glass she held out, brushing her fingers lightly as he did.

The temptation to let her fingers linger against his was crushing, so she quickly lifted her own glass to her lips. But before she could take a sip, he stopped her with his hand on her wrist.

"Here's to possibilities," he said, his voice smooth and low.

Everything inside her quivered. "To possibilities," she echoed.

They clinked glasses and, as he sampled the wine, Luke watched her over the rim. His gray eyes were dark, drawing her in. There was no use denying it to herself—she wanted him. Badly. Without losing eye contact, she sipped her drink, the cool liquid doing nothing to ease the flames that were coming to life inside her.

Luke took her wine and placed the glass next to his on the counter, then tugged her closer. And kissed her. Gently at first, the taste of wine was on his tongue, but within moments, it wasn't enough. She threaded her fingers through his hair, holding him in place, just as his hand crept up to cradle her nape. Heat shimmered between them, around them. Through her.

"Della," he murmured against her mouth. "I want you so badly I can't see straight."

With reluctance, she began to ease away, her breathing uneven. She didn't want to lead him on. He'd been nothing but patient with her—she owed it to him to play fair.

He ironed a palm down her back. "Let me turn the lights off, Della." His voice was ragged. "Let me make love to you."

A ball of panic began to rise at the base of her throat, but she swallowed it away. She wanted this. Wanted him. And for the first time in a long time, the want was more powerful than the fear.

"Yes," she whispered. Then, stronger, "Yes."

"You won't regret it, I promise." His eyes blazed as he smiled. "Even if dinner will be later than planned."

He took her hand and led her up the stairs to the bedroom. The curtains in front of the sliding door to the balcony were already drawn. He clicked a remote and the lights downstairs went out, leaving just one lamp casting a soft glow in the bedroom. In the gentle light, he resembled a fallen angel—dark blond hair framing his face, eyes brimming with temptation, strong nose and that mouth... Her breath snared high in her throat. She already knew the magic that mouth could create.

As if reading her thoughts, he kissed her lightly, then pulled away, his endless gray eyes looking deeply into hers. "Tell me if you want to stop." Another kiss, feather-light, lingering at the corner of her mouth. "But I'm telling you now, I intend to make sure you don't need to."

He clicked another button and darkness softly shrouded them. Her heart beat loudly in her ears—it was a pivotal moment in her life, that much was obvious. If she went through with this, nothing would ever be the same. But she couldn't walk away....

Standing on tippy toes, she tentatively placed her lips on his. She had to show him this was her choice—she knew what she wanted, and what she wanted was Luke. At the contact, she felt a groan reverberate in his chest but he didn't move, didn't take control of the kiss. Emboldened, she tugged on his bottom lip with her teeth and skimmed a hand up to his shoulders, tracing the muscles she'd been admiring in the kitchen earlier. Even though she couldn't see him, he filled her senses—the sound of his rough breaths, the feel of him under her fingertips, the scent of clean skin mingling with aftershave.

With an arm around her waist, he drew her closer, flush against him, and she sighed. Her body felt heavy, sweetly drugged by his kiss.

He turned her until her back was to him, leaving a trail of kisses as he went. Gently, he urged her arms up into the air, then slowly lifted her blouse. The double protection of the darkness and having him behind her allowed her to give in to the sensations and release the lurking fears. To just feel. His fingers lingered on her skin as they slid along her arms, teasing. Promising.

Her blouse swished to the floor at her feet, the delicate sound filling her awareness...until Luke's hands began their return journey from her fingertips high in the air, down her inner arms, to her sides and finally coming to rest at her waist. She almost melted in a puddle at his feet.

Hot breath warmed her ear. "I've been crazy with wanting you."

Pure sexual awareness skittered down her spine. Nothing existed but the two of them and this moment in time. Lowering her arms, she leaned back into him, reveling in the warmth, the strength of his chest supporting her. His heart thumped hard enough for her to feel and it resonated through her entire body, as if it beat just for her.

He undid the clasp on her bra, sliding the straps down her arms, and she felt the warm evening air brush across her sensitized breasts.

His hands drifted down her sides, and she tensed as his fingertips found the first bump of a scar. Saying he was fine with her marked body and discovering the reality were two different things, and she couldn't breathe as his fingers explored her ribs to her collarbone.

"Della, you're beautiful," he said, his voice rich and low.

"But the—"

He placed a finger over her lips, silencing her protest. "The scars are proof of your amazing inner strength. Enough to withstand something so awful. And that inner strength is something I find alluring. Irresistible."

With his acceptance, a shudder ran through her body and, finally, she was able to unleash the passion that had been securely locked away for far too long.

She kissed him. Hungrily. With all the wanting and needing she had for this man. And he kissed her right back, with as much passion. More.

The liquid heat of desire spread through her body. He held her waist firmly, keeping her upright, and the imprint of his hand on her bare skin burned with delicious heat.

His fingers found the zipper on her skirt and released it. The whisper of the fabric as it fell to pool at her feet was almost as erotic as Luke's touch. Almost.

His fingers slipped inside the waistband of her panties, urging them down to join her skirt on the floor. She stepped to the side, away from her clothes, and slipped out of her shoes. Never had she been as meticulously, as erotically undressed.

"And what about you," she murmured as she felt for his belt and unbuckled.

He laid his hands over hers, holding them. "I know this is selfish, but give me a few minutes to learn your body. I can't see it, so I need to explore. To discover."

Biting down hard on her bottom lip, she let go of the belt with its dangling ends and allowed Luke the time he asked for.

His head dipped, and surprisingly soft hair brushed against her throat, then her collarbone. As his hands and mouth moved across her skin, tingling awareness spread through her.

Each time his fingers found a scar, he placed a tender kiss on the flesh, and a little piece of her heart melted.

The heat of his tongue on the underside of her breast surprised her and she gasped. A hand cupped her other breast, while another snaked down her abdomen, to where she needed him the most.

Too restless with aching need to wait any longer, she reached for him. "My turn."

His body moved against hers as he straightened, then his voice was at her ear. "Our turn," he said, and dragged her lobe into his mouth.

Her knees swayed, and Luke guided her backward a step until the bed bumped into her calves. He leaned down and she heard the covers being dragged back. Then Luke's hands were at her waist again. Where they belonged. She eased down until she found the edge of the bed, then lay back, not letting go of his shoulders, bringing him with her. How had she held out against him before tonight? In this moment, he was everything she'd ever needed.

"Luke," she said, but didn't have the words to complete the sentence. To tell him everything she was experiencing.

He placed a lingering kiss on her lips, then pulled away. "Hold that thought. I'll be back in a second," he said. His body heat disappeared and there was a rustling of clothes a few feet away, followed by the sound of fabric landing on the carpet, then a drawer rolling open and a foil packet being opened.

Then he'd returned to her, his hands making the mattress dip on either side of her head. His breath, so close, sounded rough. "I've thought of little else than this moment for days."

"Me, too," she admitted.

He stilled. "I thought you didn't want this to happen."

"I didn't think it was the right thing to happen." Her hands searched for and found his face. Even though she couldn't see him, she wanted him to know this wasn't a throwaway remark, that each word was heartfelt. "I thought about it, though. Dreamed about it. About you."

"Della," he groaned.

He kissed a trail down her neck, over her collarbone and across to a breast, sending her spiraling back into his thrall. She knew his lips had passed over the puckered scars once more but she didn't care, and the moment his mouth closed over the peak of her breast, she forgot the scars altogether and lost herself in the exquisite sensations his tongue and teeth were evoking.

Greedy for it all, she touched wherever she could reach—fingertips across the crisp hair of his chest, nails lightly scraping along his abdomen, hand encircling the heaviness of his groin, eliciting a gasp from his lips.

She ached for him, needed him with a desperation that seemed only matched by his need for her. Whispering his name, she arched her hips, then whispered his name again.

When he entered her, nestling himself deep inside, her entire body quivered, overwhelmed with sensation, too much, needing more, urging him on. He moved in a steady rhythm, but she was past needing steady, so she wrapped her legs around his hips and murmured, "More."

A groan tore from his throat, and his movements became more urgent, frenzied. He hooked an elbow under her knee and lifted, changing the angle of her hips. The wave built higher, taking her up, up, until it broke, and for one perfect instant she was suspended in time and space, outside the world, and all that existed was pleasure and Luke. Then the pleasure came crashing down, filling every single fiber of her being.

And she wondered what she could ever need again.

With a final powerful thrust, he followed her over the edge, and she wrapped her arms around his shoulders tightly, wanting the moment never to end.

Minutes later, she still lay in his arms, he in hers, trembling with the intensity of what they'd shared. He'd been right—she didn't regret it. Not a single moment.

She'd taken a giant step in moving on with her life—allowing herself to become intimate with a man again. The question now was, how would she ever go back once Luke walked out of her life?

Eight

After he'd ordered two coffees, Luke looked back at Della. A small smile played around her mouth as she surveyed the view of the sweeping white beach with gentle wavelets lapping at the sand. He knew the vista from the alfresco dining area of the exclusive French restaurant in Nouméa was spectacular. But he was more interested in watching Della. She glowed, radiating serenity and happiness, and he liked to think he might be part of the reason. She was certainly responsible for how he felt—he couldn't remember ever feeling such a bone-deep contentment.

She'd come to him for the past few nights and, despite the darkness she needed to relax, their lovemaking had only grown more and more amazing.

She turned her head and her eyes met his. An easy smile curved her mouth and a jolt of awareness shook him.

"Penny?" she said.

"Nothing. Wondering…" He stopped, almost afraid of

what might come out of his mouth. He looked for a safe subject. "Tell me about growing up on ship."

"It was great." Her eyes softened. "There were advantages and disadvantages, of course, but I loved it." She looked into the distance, obviously remembering moments of her shipboard life, and he wanted to her to look back at him.

"What sort of disadvantages?"

She shrugged. "Always having to be on my very best behavior when I was outside our cabin. The lack of other children to play with."

"Did you play with the children of passengers?"

The waitress came with their coffees and after she'd left, Della turned back to him. "Sometimes, but they were few and far between. My parents mainly worked on cruise liners that were on the luxury end of the scale, catering more to couples and retired people than families. They were limited in the ships they could work on—not only did they need a ship with a vacancy for a captain and a doctor at the same time, but an owner who would allow them to bring a child. Most wouldn't."

He threaded his fingers through hers on the white linen tablecloth, loving the slide of skin that even simple hand-holding could bring. Three nights of Della Walsh weren't nearly enough to satisfy his craving for her.

Soon he'd convince her she could trust him enough to leave the lights on. She was beautiful, and seeing the same scars he'd felt under his hands wouldn't change his opinion. He wanted to watch her toffee-brown eyes when he entered her, see her face when she lost control.

Soon. He repressed a shudder of anticipation.

"Tell me about the advantages," he said.

Della took a sip of her coffee. "Seeing the world. Spending massive amounts of time with my parents. Meeting interesting people."

When he was young, he'd fantasized about an upbringing very similar to the one she described. "Did you go ashore much?"

She nodded, her eyes faraway. "My mother and I lived ashore until I was three, when my dad became a captain and could bring her back on board. After that, on school holidays, I'd often visit my cousins or grandparents. Sometimes a cousin would come to stay with us on the ship."

"You know," he said, leaning back in his chair, "I envy your childhood."

She raised her eyebrows. "You do?"

"I had a sister once. Sarah." Saying her name again was like a punch to the gut, even after all these years. Which was why he very rarely talked about her.

Della's face immediately transformed with concern. "She died?"

"When I was thirteen," he said, his tone matter of fact, as if that could counter the old pain. "Drowned at the beach."

She tightened her fingers that were still threaded with his. "Oh, Luke, I'm so sorry."

"Ironic, really," he said, one finger of his free hand rubbing the condensation on the side of his wineglass. "That the family who made their money in ships lost a daughter to the sea."

She was silent for a moment, leaving him to his own dark thoughts, until she said, "Was that when your father moved away from ships?"

"No, he'd been scared of the water since he was a kid, so as soon as he inherited, he changed his company to hotels. He didn't even want us at the beach that day, but my mother took us, anyway. When Sarah died, it just re-inforced his fears."

"Were you close to Sarah?"

He nodded. "She was only a year younger, so we spent a lot of time together."

"Oh, Luke. Her death must have hit you hard."

"Worse than hard." He cleared his throat. "And a month later, I was sent to boarding school."

A barely audible gasp slipped from her lips. "They sent you away?"

"It was a planned enrollment. They'd always meant to send me, despite my protests." At her raised eyebrow, he explained. "Before Sarah died, I'd thought they were coming around and would let me live at home through high school."

She cocked her head to the side. "After losing one child, I wouldn't have been surprised if they wanted to keep you close."

One *might* assume that. But one would be wrong.

"I wasn't the type of child they wanted to keep close." He looked out over the azure Pacific Ocean, unwilling to let the memory have a hold on him anymore.

"What do you mean?"

"Sarah was the perfect one, always instinctively know-ing how to please them." He rubbed a hand over the back of his neck. "I was…more challenging to parent."

"Let me guess," she said with an understanding smile. "You became even more challenging after losing your sister?"

He grinned. "You could say that."

Her eyes flashed in anger, but he knew it wasn't aimed at him. There was something nice about having Della on his side.

"So," she said, drawing the word out, "even though

your parents might have been softening about sending you away before Sarah died, after it happened, while you were grieving and your behavior was worse, they made you go."

The memory sat like a rock in the pit of his belly, but he wouldn't let his face betray his reaction. "That's about the crux of it, yes."

"You were just a boy." Her outrage on his behalf brought a pink flush to her alabaster cheeks. "Of *course* you were acting out."

"My parents were never particularly good at seeing things from a child's point of view," he said, his tone dry. That had to be the understatement of the year. They'd been too wrapped up in themselves and each other and barely noticed he existed.

Her eyes narrowed. "Within the space of a month, you effectively lost your entire family."

"Except Patrick," he clarified. Besides Sarah, Patrick had been his favorite family member.

She sipped her coffee, but didn't take her eyes off him. "Did you see much of him?"

"Whenever he docked in Sydney, he'd come and take me out of school for the day." Those days were some of the happiest memories of his childhood. They hadn't done anything particularly exciting, but Patrick had just had a way of making everything fun and making Luke laugh.

"Now I see why you envy my childhood—you wanted Patrick to take you out of school to live on the ship with him." She gazed at him with warm brown eyes that saw too much. He shifted in his seat, but answered truthfully.

"He told me it was impossible for a child to live on board." He'd started to wonder if Patrick had believed that, or he'd been protecting his brother who would never have consented, anyway.

"I had the childhood you wanted—growing up aboard

a ship with parents who wanted me with them. And I also lived close to Patrick for the past couple of years."

He attempted a smile. "Seems so."

"I'm sorry, Luke." She leaned closer, her gaze sincere. "That must have been hard."

With a flick of his wrist, he waved away her concern. He didn't need it. "It taught me a good lesson when I was young. Never to rely on anyone." People might promise him the world, but they never stood by him in the tough times. He had friends, sure, including his buddies from boarding school, but he would never depend on another person again, or let them close to his heart.

"What about relationships?" she asked, tucking a wayward curl behind her ear. "A good partnership needs trust. Partners need to be able to rely on each other. Surely you'd have that when you meet your soul mate?"

Soul mate? He had to cover the instinctive flinch. That was the *last* thing he wanted.

He cleared his throat. "I'm not good in relationships. I'm not interested in baring myself to another person, which they tell me is important." Though, admittedly, he couldn't remember telling anyone else the story about Sarah, or that he'd wanted to live with Patrick. Not even his ex-wife, Jillian, which probably said a whole lot about his marriage right there.

There was something about Della that made him let his guard down a bit too much. Which only meant he'd have to work extra hard to ensure neither of them got in too deep.

He tapped his fingers on the tablecloth, carefully organizing the words in his mind.

"Della," he said, capturing her gaze, "I need you to understand that anything with me can only ever be temporary." He hoped to hell she already knew it from previous conversations, but it couldn't hurt to be extra sure. And to remind himself.

Her eyelashes hid her eyes as she looked down at her hands in her lap. "So you'll always be alone?"

"It worked for Patrick, it will work just fine for me." He'd have occasional female company, and he had a strong group of friends. Alone didn't necessarily mean lonely. It meant being in control of his own life.

"Luke, have you considered that you resent the *Cora Mae?*" she asked gently. "That the person you wanted to live with as a child kept leaving you for a ship and wouldn't let you follow. And if you resent the ship, that might be behind your determination to anchor it?"

He winced. That sounded like a pile of psychobabble, but something tugged deep inside him. *Was* he trying to fulfill a boy's wish of keeping Patrick's ship chained down nearby?

He shrugged. "Who knows how the subconscious works. Either way, it also makes good business sense." He rubbed a hand across his chin. "How much do you know about floating hotels?"

"I've seen photos, heard stories."

Hearing stories and knowing specifics were poles apart. "My staff has finished working on the preliminary plans for the *Cora Mae*'s conversion and I need to review them, so I'll be flying out to Melbourne for one night. Come with me."

He'd previously considered showing her the plans his vice president was overseeing and decided there wasn't much to be gained—he was confident she would sell him all or part of her share of the ship regardless, and getting into extra detail would just muddy the waters. But something had changed. He no longer wanted her to merely sell her share of the *Cora Mae,* he wanted her to understand that this really was the best thing for the ship. To agree with him. To *want* the transformation of her home.

He cared about Della. When this was all over, he didn't want her to look back on their time together with bad feelings, or to think she'd somehow lost. He'd like to think she'd remember him fondly. This situation with the ship needed to be resolved in a win-win. Della had to be convinced his plan was for the best.

She chewed on her bottom lip. "When?"

He did a few mental calculations about flight times and their next ports of call. "How much notice do you need to give the medical department to get another doctor to cover you?"

"Depends on how quickly we find one." A frown line appeared between her brows. "But I'm not sure what this would achieve—I already understand the concept."

He placed his upturned palms on the table. "I've given you the commitment of three weeks and an open mind while you tried to convince me that your plans for the *Cora Mae* are best. It's a reasonable expectation that you would do the same. I don't even need the three weeks. Just a couple of days."

She blew out a breath and nodded. "I'll make some inquiries with the doctors who cover for Cal and my holidays, and see when they're available."

"I appreciate that." His shoulders relaxed. He was surer than ever that this was the best plan for everyone. Convince her the *Cora Mae* would be better as a floating hotel, and do it quickly, before either of them formed an emotional attachment to the other.

That night, Della went back to Luke's cabin after dinner. They'd been invited to dine at the captain's table, and had agreed that their intimate relationship should stay private while so much rested on their negotiations about the *Cora Mae*. So she'd sat through the torture of not being able to touch him through an entire meal.

Well, more precisely, they hadn't touched where anyone else could see. But those long white tablecloths were excellent cover for questing hands.

"Coffee?" he asked, his eyes betraying a lack of interest in the drink.

"No, thanks." She bit down on a smile, but it escaped, anyway.

He loosened his tie. "Tea? Wine?"

"Nope." She took two steps closer, until she was within touching distance.

"So, there's nothing you want?" he asked mildly.

Her hands rested on his chest, reveling in the solidness beneath the crisp white shirt. "Oh, there's something I want. Something I've been desperate for all night."

"They'll serve anything you ask for at the captain's table," he said, one hand cupping her cheek. "What could you have possibly wanted that they couldn't provide?"

"This." And she kissed him, slowly, thoroughly, the way she'd been dreaming of since they'd sat down at dinner. Her conversations with passengers and other crew had probably been muddled, given that most of her focus had remained on the man who sat beside her, no matter who she was talking to. All she'd wanted to do was this. Just this.

Without breaking the kiss, he lifted her into his arms and carried her up the stairs to the bedroom, letting her slide down his body just inside the door.

She leaned into his neck, inhaling the scent of him as she caught her breath. "Nice move, Luke."

"Here's another one." He walked her back a step until

her shoulders bumped against the wall. "Now kiss me again."

She lifted her face and met his mouth with hers, showing him all the passion that welled up inside her when he was near.

"Della," he said, his voice ragged. "I want to see you when I make love to you."

Her blood turned to ice. Didn't he realize how impossible that was for her? Tension flowed into her limbs, the rigidness almost painful after the lovely lassitude of only moments ago.

Slowly, she withdrew her arms and wrapped them around her waist. "Isn't what we have enough?"

"What we've shared has been amazing." He leaned in, his lips so close to her ear that she could feel the warmth of his breath. "But I want to see your face when you slide over the edge. I want you to see me when I'm inside you."

Her eyes drifted closed, imagining the scene he described. She'd do almost anything to be able to see his face in those moments, too. *Almost* anything. But certainly not what he asked.

She turned her head and focused on the night sky through the window. "I'm sorry, Luke, I just can't."

With a finger, he turned her face until his eyes filled her vision again. "You don't think I can handle the way your body looks," he said softly, but with an undercurrent of accusation. Perhaps even hurt.

"If I'm…"

"Exposed," he supplied.

She nodded, accepting his word choice. It was important he understood that this was no whim, that what he asked was simply not possible. "I won't be able to relax. I'd be too self-conscious to enjoy what we were doing."

She saw understanding dawn in his eyes and began to relax.

"Okay, new plan," he said and gently touched his lips to the tip of her nose. "Leave the dress on."

He kissed her again, tenderly, and while she was distracted, he slid his hands up under her skirt, lingering over the satiny skin of her inner thighs, then hooked his thumbs in the elastic of her lacy panties, peeling them down.

"You'll leave my dress on?" she asked warily, watching his progress with removing her underwear.

"I swear." He lifted one of her feet, then the other, so she could step out of her panties. "It's not my preferred option, but at least I'll be able to see your face."

The possibility unfolded before her like a shining jewel. If she could trust him to keep his word, she'd be able to see him during those intimate moments, to connect with him on a deeper level, to watch his release. Her pulse began to race.

As Luke stood, she wrapped her arms around his neck. "If I'm consenting to the lights on, do I get a reward?"

"What do you want?" he asked with a lazy smile.

She undid the knot in his tie and slid it out from his collar, then threw it across the room. "All your clothes come off."

"That's hardly fair," he said, chuckling. "I'll keep one item, like you are. And technically you have two, since there's a bra under that dress."

"Nope, they all come off." She touched her tongue to her top lip, and watched him watch the action. "In exchange for the lights."

He blinked slowly, the corners of his mouth twitching. "You drive a hard bargain."

"And they come off now. Before we start."

A slow, lazy smile spread across his face. "I need to

watch you closer next time we discuss the *Cora Mae*. You have hidden negotiating talents." But he stepped back and quickly dispensed with his shoes, socks, trousers and shirt.

She reached out, letting her fingers dance across his skin. With the lights out the past few nights, she'd been blocked from seeing his body. Such a shame considering the shape of him. She'd seen his bare chest the day they'd swum at the Bay of Islands, but seeing it up close, being able to touch it… A hot shiver ran down her spine.

"And the rest," she said, her voice uneven. "My underwear's already gone."

"I've changed my mind." He stepped forward, pushing her back into the wall, and claimed her mouth. The kiss was hot, demanding, and she gave herself completely to its power. His hands roamed down her sides, exploring her curves beneath the fabric but leaving the dress in place as he'd promised.

He wrenched his mouth away and rested his forehead against hers, their breath mingling. "I can't wait to see more of you," he whispered.

With hands that moved an inch ahead of his mouth, he made his way along the line of her jaw, down her throat. Pausing at the sensitive place where her neck sloped into her shoulders, he gently abraded her skin with his teeth, sending sparks of desire through her system.

Unable to reach much of him as he dipped lower, she moved impatiently, stroking from the strong column of his throat down to his biceps. When his knees touched the ground, he looked up, the whole world in his eyes. Nothing could have prevented her from smiling down at him.

He gripped one of her ankles and slid a shoe off, followed by the other, then his hands slid up her legs, spreading them a little farther apart as he went. Finding the hem of her dress, he bunched it in his fingers and kept on traveling, exposing new flesh inch by inch. When he reached the juncture of her thighs, his hands trapped her hips firmly against the wall, and he placed a delicate kiss there. Then his tongue flicked out and found the core of her. A moan ripped from her throat, just as his lips joined in.

Her breathing choppy, she managed a mangled version of "please," not sure exactly what she was asking for. Luke continued his work regardless, his tongue circling and sweeping, driving her slowly crazy. She dug her nails into the muscles of his shoulders, needing something to anchor herself as her bones melted into nothingness.

His hands pushed her harder against the wall, his mouth merciless. She writhed, arms flung out to the wall behind her, hands looking for purchase as reality dissolved.

"Luke," she gasped, then pleasure pulsed sharply through her and she imploded.

He moved up her body until he stood, holding her against him, supporting her as she came back to earth. When she could breathe again, she opened her eyes to find him looking at her.

"Thank you," he murmured.

She coughed out a laugh. "I should be thanking you."

"Feel free," he said and grinned. "But I was thanking you for trusting me in the light."

She ran her hands over his bare shoulders, luxuriating in the polished smoothness. "I'm glad I did."

"Mmm, I think that should be, *I'm glad I* am *trusting you, Luke,*" he said, using a hand under her knee to lift her leg and wrap it around his hips.

A shiver raced across her skin. "Oh, yes. I *am,* Luke. And I'll be glad for as long as you want me to."

He dug his fingers under the waistband of his boxer

shorts and came out with a little foil packet that he presented to her with a flourish. "Excellent."

She looked down at the waistband of his boxers then back to his face. "How long have you had that in there?"

"About a minute and a half." He pushed the underwear down his legs and kicked it away. "I dug it out of my trousers just before I stood up."

"I like a man who thinks ahead," she said as she took it from his fingers. Pushing him back an inch to give herself some room, she ripped the packet open and rolled the protection along his length.

"You also might like this." He lifted her and wrapped her other leg around his hips so she could lock her ankles behind him. Only the thin cotton of her dress bunched around her hips lay between them.

"Like?" she said on a gasp. "This is fast becoming one of my favorite things."

His hands supported her, positioned her, and as she felt the tip of him seeking entrance, her eyes drifted closed.

Luke stilled. "Open your eyes," he said, his voice deep and rough.

She lifted her lids and found his gray eyes locked on her. "Better," he murmured. "I'm not missing out this time on seeing your eyes when we're joined."

He began to move again, small movements, merely nudging her, building anticipation until she couldn't stand it any longer. She braced her back on the wall behind her and reached down to find him, then guided him into her as she sank down.

Air hissed out from between his teeth, but he didn't lose eye contact.

The feel of him filling her while watching his face in the fully lit room made something shift in her chest. The times they'd made love in the dark she'd known it was him, of course she had, but perhaps there had been some little corner of her brain that had played dumb, thinking if she didn't see him she wasn't breaking the vows she'd once made to her husband.

But here and now there was no denying this was Luke she had her thighs wrapped around. Luke thrusting into her. Luke with his fingers biting into the flesh of her hips as he moved her to his rhythm. And she didn't want anyone else. Only him. Only ever Luke.

"Della," he groaned, his body vibrating with tension. He changed the angle of her hips and sparks shot through her entire body. Driving her fingers through his hair, she dragged his mouth down to hers.

He kissed her hungrily, then pulled his mouth back a couple of inches, and she took the chance to fill her screaming lungs. His chest heaved in and out, but his gaze didn't waver. Taking her higher, higher, to a place just out of reach, higher. Luke was whispering, eyes still on her, telling her she was beautiful, that she drove him crazy with want, saying her name. Then she burst free. Free of everything but this man. Within moments, Luke convulsed in her arms, his eyes only closing in the final moments of his pleasure.

Minutes—hours?—later, he released her legs and they stumbled to the bed. Despite her exhaustion, a joy deep down bubbled away and she snuggled against his side, completely relaxed. Supremely content.

Yet, as she lay in Luke's embrace, a dark cloud moved over her heart. Was she falling in love? Her skin grew cold. For everyone's sakes, she hoped not—despite being a good man, Luke had told her today in Nouméa that he didn't want a true relationship. He wouldn't *want* to be loved. And after experiencing the utter devastation that could come from loving someone, she would never open

herself to the possibility again. If she let herself love Luke
and she lost him, if he left her, it would kill her.

Glancing up at Luke's strong profile as he dozed, she
mercilessly squashed down the joy that had been building. She simply wouldn't let herself love him. She'd enjoy
all he had to offer, then leave with her heart intact when
they parted. Simple.

The dark cloud continued to hover, making a mockery
of her naïveté, but she determinedly ignored it and nuzzled
in closer to her lover's side.

Nine

Three days later, Luke unlocked the front door to his Melbourne penthouse apartment and ushered Della inside. Fortunately, one of the doctors who often covered for Della's and Cal's holidays had been available to meet the ship and fill in, so Luke had quickly arranged their trip to his hometown. It was only fair that she could see what he wanted to transform the *Cora Mae* into before she made her decision.

They'd flown in from Samoa this morning and he'd spent the afternoon at his office. He'd wanted the time to sign contracts and other paperwork that had been waiting for him while he was cruising the South Pacific—to clear his plate so he could devote tomorrow to Della and the *Cora Mae*.

Della had spent the afternoon with her parents before Luke had picked her up and brought her back to his home. He'd only spoken to her parents briefly, but he'd liked them, and knowing they'd been friends of Patrick's made him like them all the more.

He pulled his front door shut behind him and carried his and Della's bags through to the main bedroom, rolling his shoulders to ease the tension. All the good effects from his time on the *Cora Mae* had dissipated the moment he'd stepped back into the Marlow Hotels office and the weight of responsibility had come crashing back down.

When he came back, Della was standing near his sofa, taking in the room. "This doesn't seem very…lived in," she said.

Loosening his tie, he glanced around his living room. "I don't spend much time here. Most of my day is at the office, and I usually spend time off with friends. Also I travel a fair bit, checking on the hotels."

Della drifted across to the floor-to-ceiling windows that showcased the city below. Twilight had descended and Melbourne was bathed in its magical glow. It was his favorite time of day, and one of the reasons he'd bought the apartment.

Yet it was the woman standing in front of the window who claimed his attention. He crossed to her, wrapped his arms around her waist from behind and glanced at the view over her shoulder. The feel of her against him brought a satisfaction to his blood that he never would have predicted.

"It's beautiful," she said, leaning her head back on to his shoulder.

"Not as beautiful as you." Gently, he turned her in his arms and captured her lips, his heart beating faster from the simple kiss. "I'm looking forward to making love to you in my bed," he murmured. A primal, possessive need deep down inside him wanted to make love to her here, in his home.

She shivered and smiled. "That's a plan I can agree to."

"But first, I'll feed you," he said on a sigh, and pulled away from her special brand of temptation. "I'm afraid my cooking skills are confined to breakfast, so we'll have to order in."

She blinked at him. "You cook breakfast?"

"Omelets, scrambled eggs with grilled tomatoes, pancakes—I have a full repertoire. Just no dinner." Partly because he was rarely home for dinner. "Have a look through the menus beside the phone and choose anything you'd like. I just need to check a couple of things."

He'd been working while aboard the ship, though not as many hours a day as he'd usually put in, and the pile of work waiting for him today was evidence that he'd relaxed a bit too much. That had to end.

As he opened his laptop and waited for it to fire up, his gaze was drawn back to Della. She was in his kitchen, ringing the local Indian takeout. Something shifted in his chest. She looked good there.

He'd never had a woman in his apartment before; he didn't like the complications it brought. The expectations it might engender. But Della was different. Mainly because he knew she didn't want a life on the land, so she wasn't thinking she could turn him into a long-term prospect.

He rubbed a hand over his jaw. No, it was more. There was something about Della herself. Her presence made him feel different inside. Perhaps it was that he could be more himself with her. She—

Heart fisted tight, he stopped himself before he could get carried away. He didn't need a woman to make him feel *anything*. He didn't need anyone.

He repeated his golden rule under his breath. *Never be distracted by a woman; never rely on anyone.*

They were lovers, and he would have her in his bed

tonight, but he wouldn't indulge in any flights of fancy about what they had together.

Della Walsh was temporary in his life.

Della ended the call and watched Luke as his fingers flew over his laptop keyboard. Despite his words being just as considerate, and the reaction he caused in her body just as strong, this wasn't the same man tonight as the man she'd known on the ship.

He didn't even look the same—there was more tension in his shoulders, his back was a fraction straighter. There was a touch more arrogance in the angle he held his head. It had begun when they'd landed in Melbourne, and had been more pronounced when he'd picked her up after her late lunch with her parents. In fact, the effect was growing stronger every minute they spent in this city.

This was Luke the businessman, the man she'd met after Patrick's will reading who'd been determined to get her half of the ship for himself. The man she'd slapped, she remembered, biting down on her lip.

Somewhere during their time together, he'd relaxed and stopped regarding her as the enemy. He'd become the man who treated her with tenderness, who had been patient about her scarred body and who laughed with her over mini golf.

Which man was the real Luke—tense businessman or relaxed lover?

He glanced up, saw her watching him and gave her a tight smile, then went back to his laptop. Embarrassed at being caught staring, she started going through his cupboards, pulling out plates and cutlery for the food that would soon be on its way. But her thoughts wouldn't be so easily diverted.

It wasn't unusual for people to act out of character on

vacation, which was what their time on the *Cora Mae* had practically become. It was why holiday flings were renowned for not lasting. An unwelcome thought that she'd been ignoring finally surfaced—it was more than two weeks since Luke had made the deal to consider keeping the *Cora Mae* as a cruising vessel, but he didn't seem to be coming around. What if he'd been stringing her along? Her stomach swooped. Perhaps he'd been pretending to be considering her wishes, charming her into trusting him, entertaining them both with a fling.

Maybe there weren't two Lukes, there was just this one, the focused businessman. And the man she'd come to know on the ship had been a role he was playing, either intentionally or because he'd been caught up in his holiday.

Had she fallen in love with a mirage?

Love…

Oh, no. Oh, God. She'd promised herself she wasn't falling in love with him. With trembling hands, she placed the crockery and cutlery carefully on his dining table.

Love…?

He shut down his laptop, stretched his arms above his head and stood. Then he cast a lazy smile across at her and her insides melted.

"How long until the food arrives?" he asked.

She swallowed, trying to keep her wits about her. "Thirty minutes."

"Enough time to show you my bed." He prowled closer, encircled her in his arms. "Come with me," he whispered beside her ear then pulled her lobe into the warmth of his mouth.

Heat shimmered across her skin. This was desire, not love. A holiday fling that would end soon. As long as she kept treating it that way, it was no threat to her heart.

She ran her hands up his solid chest. "We'd have to be quick."

"I can still make it worth your while," he said with a devilish gleam in his gray eyes.

She let him lead her down a hallway, determined to enjoy whatever time she could have with whichever Luke this was. Because it wouldn't be long before she lost him completely.

The next morning, Della stepped into the boardroom that adjoined Luke's office and glanced around. Since they were only a few blocks from his apartment building, the floor-to-ceiling windows held a similar view of the bustling city below, and the decor had the same impersonal feel. The difference was that it felt right in a business environment.

Though she'd suspected his life was dominated by his career, so perhaps it was appropriate that his home reflected his office.

"Coffee?" Luke asked, heading for a small table against the wall, lavishly laid out with coffee and tea, iced biscuits, fresh pastries and tiny cakes.

"Are we expecting a hoard?"

"Just us, though we can call in the people who worked on this project if we have questions." He glanced at the catering table. "My assistant always stocks the room if people will be working in here."

"Just coffee, then," she said and strolled over to the plans strewn across the boardroom table. There were detailed diagrams of waste management systems, power generators and water production. High piles of reports sat to the side, with an environmental impact report sitting at the top of the pile closest to her. Projected on a huge white screen was a slideshow of artists' renditions of the *Cora Mae* in her new surroundings of the Great Barrier Reef.

Luke handed her a mug of steaming coffee, then pointed to the sailors' quarters on the main plans. "As you can see, these rooms will be converted to a permanent research facility for marine biologists and other scientists. We'd also employ a full-time environmental scientist to ensure the impact on the reef is minimized."

"Interesting," she murmured as she continued to peruse the plans. They were details she hadn't expected him to consider and was pleasantly surprised to see them included.

A couple of hours and another cup of coffee later, she'd had a chance to flick through most of the presentation. Luke rested a hip on the edge of the table and crossed his arms. "Well, what do you think?"

"To be honest, it's not as bad as I was expecting," she admitted.

He cocked his head. "What were you expecting?"

"I'm not sure." She glanced up at the screen projection of the *Cora Mae* on the wall. "Maybe something akin to a caged bird."

"And now?" he asked, leaning infinitesimally forward.

"By being permanently anchored, she's part of her surroundings." She looked back to Luke, surprised at the direction of her own thoughts. "She belongs, instead of just passing through."

Luke nodded. "That permanency also means the crew would have the option of living on board as they do now, or having a home base on the coast and working a roster of several days on at a time. They wouldn't have to make the decisions that your parents did when you were first born. You would have all stayed together as a family."

"Ah, but then I would have missed out on the travel,"

she said, feeling nostalgia pull her lips into a smile. "The amazing learning experiences that most other children just aren't able to access."

He sank into a seat beside hers, curiosity in his eyes. "Like what?"

She pushed her chair out a few feet and stretched her legs as the memories crowded into her mind. "When I was twelve, we were on the *Mediterranean Queen,* and my mother planned my homeschooling projects around Ancient Greece and Rome. We studied the civilizations when we were out to sea, then walked the ruins and historical sites on the days in port."

He regarded her for a long moment, tapping a finger on his thigh as he did. "You know, you guessed when we were in Nouméa that, in some ways, you'd had the childhood I'd wanted—growing up on a ship, all the time you spent with Patrick in the last few years. And you were right. But it was also the polar opposite of the childhood I had—you experienced the freedom, the travel, while I was in boarding school day and night."

"Like a caged bird," she said softly.

His gaze drifted to the expanse of glass along one wall, but she didn't think his focus was on the view. "I think part of me probably did feel like that at the time."

"And when you talked about that in Nouméa, I asked if you resented the *Cora Mae,* and if that was affecting your decision about her future."

He nodded as he turned back to her. "I said I didn't know."

"What if it's not about resentment?" she asked tentatively. At his quizzical expression, she rolled her bottom lip between her teeth and carefully chose the words to explain. "I'm wondering how that childhood of being cooped up, of having no freedoms, no real holidays, would affect a person. Would it make them want to take a ship that traveled, that was free, and chain it down to one spot?"

He rubbed a hand over his jaw. "Perhaps. And I wonder how a person who'd grown up with a vast experience of travel, of always moving, would feel about a ship being permanently anchored? Especially if that person's one proper experience of life in one place ended in tragedy. Would they see it as an emotional issue, maybe even transfer their own fears on to the ship?"

She felt the corners of her mouth tug into a smile as she acknowledged his point. "Probably."

He chuckled. "We're a fine pair."

For a precious moment it was as if the veil of businessman had lifted and the Luke she'd known on the *Cora Mae* had reemerged. Her heart lifted, and she found the courage to ask a question that had been playing at the corners of her mind. "Do you mind if I ask something personal?"

He arched an eyebrow. "There's something more personal than analyzing my childhood and its effects on present-day business decisions?"

She smiled, then sobered. "Patrick often talked about you, so I knew a few things about you before we met. Yet some things you never mention."

He shrugged his broad shoulders. "Ask what you want to know."

"You were married," she said simply.

His expression was carefully schooled to neutral. "I was."

"You've never mentioned an ex-wife." She would have had no idea he'd been married if not for Patrick's family stories.

"It's never come up in conversation," he said smoothly and picked up the report nearest his hand.

Instinct told her to back off, but she didn't want to let it go and risk never knowing about his romantic past. "True. Yet you've mentioned that your sister died when you were thirteen, and I've talked about having been married. We've both been pretty open with each other."

"Are you saying I've deliberately avoided mentioning my ex-wife?"

She held his gaze. "Have you?"

"Perhaps," he acknowledged, and tossed the report back onto the table. "I try to avoid thinking about her if I can."

"Why?"

"Mainly because it makes me look like a fool," he said with a self-deprecating smile.

"When Patrick talked about your marriage—" she hesitated, then plunged in "—he always seemed to be angry but he never said why."

A humorless laugh puffed from his throat. "He saw through her from the start."

"What happened?"

He eased out a long breath. "She worked at Marlow Corporation, but apparently decided that it would be an easier life to marry the boss than to work for him."

Her heart clenched tight, aching for him. "She was using you?"

"From day one."

Suddenly several things made sense—his comments about insincere compliments the day they first went to meet Roxie Appleby in the galley. His suspicions about her influencing Patrick to leave her half the ship…

"Just so you know," she said slowly, "I wasn't doing that with Patrick."

He reached over and took her hand, lacing their fingers. "I realized that a while ago. Besides, I should have had more faith in Patrick's ability to size people up—he wouldn't have stood for you trying to manipulate him, even if he was sick. He was always stubborn and a particularly good judge of character."

She'd assumed Luke wouldn't be sleeping with her had he continued to believe she'd used her position to influence his uncle, but it was still a weight off her shoulders to hear him say the words. She nudged her chair over beside his and laid her head on his shoulder. He rested an arm around her shoulders.

"You know," she murmured, "you were Patrick's favorite person."

There was silence for so long she thought he wasn't going to reply. "I should have visited more," he finally said, his voice rough around the edges.

She turned, found his gaze. "He knew you'd come if he wanted you, Luke."

Tenderly, he stroked a finger down her cheek. "I'm glad you were there for him. That he had someone with your heart and your skills with him at the end."

Tears pressed at the back of her eyes. He'd given her a gift.

He leaned in and softly touched his mouth to hers, with more emotion than she thought could fit in one simple kiss. And then she knew for sure—there was no use denying any longer.

She loved this man. Loved him so much it lifted her up until she was floating.

And, though she knew it would lead to pain and grief all over again, in this moment she couldn't bring herself to care. All she needed right now was Luke. She threaded her arms behind his neck and kissed him again.

Ten

Della arrived at the medical suites for her morning shift only half an hour after leaving Luke's cabin. They'd been back on board for two days, spending every spare moment together, usually in his bed. Luke had begun to relax again once they'd boarded the *Cora Mae* in Fiji, which was great, but her own immense relief to be back on the ship had been uncomfortably surprising.

"Good morning, Dr. Walsh. Sleep well?" Jody asked. The twinkle in her eye made Della wince. Apparently the *Cora Mae*'s rumor mill was in fine working order—she'd wondered if she and Luke had been able to keep their involvement a secret, or if word was seeping out. Now she had her answer.

"Fine, thank you." Della picked up the log of calls taken since the medical suite had been open yesterday and perused it, both to keep an eye on things and to cover for any potential blushing. "How about you?"

Jody shrugged theatrically. "You know how it is. One of my roommates came in late, and another one snored, so it was hard to get some sleep." She straightened the pens on her desk then stopped and looked up at Della. "Oh, no, that's right. You wouldn't know, since you have a cabin to yourself. No one there to wake you. All on your own. All night."

Della smothered a chuckle as she put down the log book and crossed her arms. "Is there something you're trying to say, Jody?"

"No, no." Jody smiled sweetly. "Why, is there something you want to share?"

Della tapped a pen against her lips. Perhaps it would help her sort through the mess of her emotions if she talked about it with someone. She'd known Jody a couple of years and she trusted her.

Before she could decide, a call came through on the emergency line. Jody tapped a button and said, "Medical suite."

"This is the bridge. Medical team needed to Galley Two immediately. A fire has been reported. Fire teams on their way and warning about to go out to all passengers. Medical assessment and first-aid station required."

Della had already swung into action, grabbing one of the first-aid backpacks that were stored in a cupboard near the door. "On our way," Jody said, as she hung up and grabbed a second backpack.

The door to the suite opened and their other nurse, Maree, came in. Della paused just long enough to say, "Fire in Galley Two. Page Cal then meet us down there," before she and Jody slipped outside. Della's pulse was fast and erratic. Fire was a ship's worst enemy and she had no idea of the scale of what they were about to face. With any luck it would be small and already contained.

As they ran along the corridors and down the stairs, a calm message came over the P.A. system advising passengers that there was a small fire in one of the kitchens, and as a precaution Section Four of the ship would be evacuated until the fire teams declared it safe to return.

Thankfully, it was midmorning on a day in port, and most of the passengers would already be sightseeing in the New Zealand capital, Wellington. Passengers all received a solid briefing on emergencies when they first boarded, but this would be a heck of a lot simpler with most of them ashore.

They reached the closed doors that marked the edge of Section Four. Max, a steward from the premium suites, was standing guard. In the event of a fire, crew members had assigned roles—everyone was part of the emergency plans and fire drills.

"What have we got, Max?" she asked, slightly out of breath. She took in the small crowd of galley staff who had been evacuated from the exclusion zone.

Three more crew members rushed down the corridor, still adjusting their helmets, and Max stepped aside to let them through as he answered.

"The first team hasn't been in long, but the fire seems to be contained to Galley Two. There's an office on the left you can use as a first-aid station."

"Thanks." Della and Jody dropped their backpacks just as a few more of the galley staff were led out through the doors, looking a little dazed. Max pointed them to Della and she and Jody got to work checking them for burns and smoke inhalation.

Another group of galley staff emerged just as Cal came through the door and grabbed a pair of surgical gloves. "Where do you want me?"

Della looked up from dressing a minor burn on a chef's

forearm. "Check the office next door. If it's got room, take Maree and start a second station."

"Roger." Cal disappeared with Maree, then reappeared and invited some of the lined-up galley crew to the second room. Della grabbed a rubber band from the desk in the office and put her hair up. The air-conditioning would have been turned off in the next section by now and even on this side of the wall it was warming up.

More people trickled in, some coughing—most had breathed smoke before they'd made it out and many had minor burns as they'd tried to contain the fire. The smell of smoke and fire lingered in the air, but no one was panicking—they trained regularly for this.

She was confident in the fire crew's ability, but fire was unpredictable and potentially devastating, and so many people seemed to have been affected. This place was her home; the people were her second family. She sent up a little prayer that no one had been hurt badly—the only concession she could afford to make to the anxiety that crept through her—and kept working.

"What can I do?" The voice was deep and calm behind her. She turned to see Luke, so tall and solid and unflappable, and suddenly she felt centered again. "Do you have first-aid training?"

"Advanced first aid, updated every year."

"Excellent. Grab a pair of gloves from Jody. You can take her seat. Jody, there are more people coming through—can you go out and start assessing and prioritizing those waiting?"

"On it," the nurse said and vacated her seat for Luke.

Working beside him was smooth and easy—they immediately slipped into a routine where she passed him patients who only needed basic attention and he followed her instructions without question. There was a synergy to their work.

Della looked up for her next patient and saw Roxie Appleby. "Roxie, how are you?"

"Just a little burn on my wrist," she said and sat in the chair.

"Let me have a look." Della took her hand, noting that it was only a mild burn. "Did you see how the fire started?"

Roxie sighed. "It was a few stations across from me. I didn't see, but it spread fairly quickly and we all rushed to smother it with the fire blankets. A couple of cooks grabbed the fire extinguishers and the sprinklers came on, but it's still going on in there."

"I'm glad you weren't hurt more than this. Once we're done here, I want you to go up to the top deck and get some fresh air. The people we've seen will already be up there." She turned to Luke. "Luke, can you get Roxie some oxygen while I do a dressing on her burn?"

"Not a problem," Luke said, then started talking to Roxie in soothing tones as Della dressed the burn.

They worked side by side for another ten minutes before Max rushed in and squatted beside Della. "Dr. Walsh, they need you in there. They have a chef collapsed and they want your okay before they move him. He has some burns."

Della nodded and her stomach sank as she mentally ran through all the chefs she knew but hadn't seen in the first-aid station yet. "Have you got a fire suit for me?"

"Yep, over here," Max said as they walked to the door. She felt Luke move beside her. "I'll come with you."

His reassuring presence and extra pair of hands would be valuable but she couldn't accept his offer. "It's policy not to take noncrew into a fire zone." She gave him a tight smile as she took the heavy orange suit from Max. "I'll be fine."

"Dr. Walsh," he said, sounding every inch the powerful businessman he was. "I'm a half-owner of the ship and I have an advanced first-aid certificate. You might need help and you can't spare one of the nurses from here."

She bit down on her lip as she considered. He was right—being half-owner of the ship probably meant the policy didn't apply to him. "Are you sure?"

"Absolutely." Luke's steel-gray gaze didn't waver.

Della nodded. "Jody, you'll need to take over in here, and call in a couple of the crew with first-aid training. Mr. Marlow and I are going into the galley."

She pulled the suit on over her clothes, finishing with the helmet, as Luke did the same, then they made their way into the exclusion zone, Luke carrying a stretcher. Once on the other side of the door, Luke gave her fingers a squeeze and she threw him a grateful smile.

It was dark and hot—all electricity had been turned off, but their helmets had torches and they found their way easily enough through the other rooms in Section Four till they reached the galley. Soot covered the countertops and the food that had been in the process of being prepared, and fire retardant foam was piled high in places where the fire team had worked. Even with the air filter on her helmet, she could smell the smoke in the air.

She weaved through the benches until one of the crew in an orange suit and helmet waved her over and guided her to the collapsed man he'd been sitting with. Della knelt down beside the dazed but conscious chef, who was wearing an oxygen mask and a white uniform with scorch marks. She only vaguely recognized him, and double-checked his badge to find his name was Ted before she said, "Hi, Ted. It's Dr. Walsh. You've had a fall, but you'll be fine now."

She listened to his breathing and felt for his pulse. While Luke spoke reassuringly to the man, she continued the assessment, including looking for any damage that may have occurred when he fell. He had some burns, but she was more worried about his lungs, given the smoke he must have breathed in before the fire crew had fitted the mask. Luckily, he didn't appear to have hurt himself much when he collapsed, so she gave the okay to move him. The three of them rolled the man onto a stretcher, then she and Luke carried him out.

As soon as they made it out the door and through the line of galley staff that snaked its way along the corridor, Max grabbed the handles from her end of the stretcher, and she whipped off her mask, relief sweeping through her that the worst was probably over.

"Jody, call the city hospital," she said as she stripped off her fire suit. "We need an ambulance urgently."

Jody reached for the phone and gave instructions to the ship's operator. Della hung her fire suit over a chair, then took the handles from Luke so he could get out of his. "We need to take him up to the lobby. I'll do some first aid there, so at least we're ready for the ambulance when it arrives. Are you all right to keep carrying him?"

"Yep," he said, and took his end back.

"Max, can you get someone else to carry the other end—I need to keep my hands free. Also, someone to run to the medical suite to pick up some supplies." She grabbed one of the first-aid backpacks from the doorway. "Jody, can you travel in the ambulance with him?"

"Sure," the nurse said.

Della ducked her head into Cal's makeshift first-aid room. "Maree, we're going to need you to take over in the other room—Jody's going with the ambulance. I'll be back down as soon as I can. Jody's already called in more first aiders to help you both. They should be arriving any minute."

The rest of the day passed in a blur. Della heard from Jody when she returned a couple of hours later that the chef was doing well at the hospital.

They treated more crew—the galley had been full of chefs, cooks and waitstaff serving late breakfasts and prepping for lunch, and everyone needed at least a quick check over. Luckily no one else was hurt as badly as the chef taken ashore, and everything could be handled by the *Cora Mae*'s medical team. Luke worked like a Trojan on any task she set him, and handed her a bottle of water and a smile each time she turned around.

Once the last person had been seen, Della was tired and desperately needed a shower, but began the cleanup in the office where they'd had the first-aid station.

Luke laid a hand on her shoulder and looked into her eyes. "Can the others handle the cleanup without you?"

She glanced around at the rest of the team, plus the other first aiders Jody had called in. They'd all had a long day.

"They could," she said, turning back to him, "but I don't want to leave it all to them."

"You won't be slacking off. Captain Tynan wants to see us both as soon as we're free."

"Go," Cal said. "I'd rather do the cleanup with Jody and Maree than go to the logistics meeting you're about to have."

"Okay, thanks," she said on a sigh and followed Luke out the door.

As they walked along the corridors, Luke draped an

arm over her shoulders. She glanced up at him and he shrugged. "I'm pretty sure the crew all know we're seeing each other, so why shouldn't I give you a bit of support after the day you've put in?"

She thought back to Jody's comments that morning and smiled. "I think they know, too." And it felt good—right—to walk along, physically linked to the man she loved.

Yet a shiver raced across her skin. They hadn't talked about it, but they both knew their time together was coming to an end. And despite the darkened surroundings that she still insisted on when their clothes were off, there had been more intimacy, and a sense of urgency to their love-making since they'd come back from Melbourne. As if each time could be their last.

And once that last time inevitably happened, she wasn't sure how she'd bear it.

When they reached the meeting room, she followed Luke over to where the captain and several key senior crew members were gathered.

Captain Tynan looked up from the ship plans that were spread over the table. "Ah, Mr. Marlow, Dr. Walsh. Excellent. This will be easier with you both here. That was the advantage of Patrick living on board, too—on other ships I'd have to ring the head office to get authorization for significant repairs."

Della chewed on her lip. When she'd talked to Patrick about the running of the ship, they'd discussed big picture topics like routes and entertainments, not issues like repairs. She'd need to pay attention to this discussion to keep up.

Like a man used to being in charge, Luke strode to the captain's side and ran a hand over the detailed plans. "What do we know of the damage so far?"

The captain tapped a pen on the table in a rapid rhythm. "Obviously we haven't been able to do a thorough analysis of the affected areas yet, but from reports the fire officers gave in their debriefing, we can make some rough guesses."

"Bad?" Luke asked, glancing up at the other man.

"We don't think any of the ship's structure has been compromised, thanks in large part to the actions of the galley crew and the fire officers. The damage seems to be localized to Galley Two." The captain pointed to the area on the plans. Since she wasn't sure what to say, Della leaned over to look, despite knowing the layout of the ship like the back of her hand.

Luke straightened and crossed his arms over his chest. "Can the other galleys take on the work of Galley Two while the repairs are carried out?"

"With some changes to scheduling, yes." The captain pointed out the other galleys on the plans. "And the menu options for the premium cabins can be restricted to allow their galley to take on a larger load."

"Excellent," Luke said, obviously satisfied with the plan. "It's fortunate we're in port, so we can get access to materials and tradesmen straight away."

"And that both co-owners can give authorization to the expenses straight away, since this will likely exceed my budget."

Exceed the captain's budget? She had no idea if the *Cora Mae* had more money in reserve. Why hadn't she thought to ask that after the will reading?

Luke moved to the other side of the table to get a closer look at something on the plan. "How soon do the fire officers expect it'll be until we can get in to do a thorough assessment of the damage so we can make firm plans?"

Della kept listening to the exchange among Luke, the

captain and the senior crew, but her heart was sinking. Damages, repair costs and contingency plans. What did she know of such things? She knew about smoke inhalation, burns, fatigue and dehydration, but in this conversation she was completely superfluous.

Luckily, Luke knew what he was doing. He handled the staff and the plans like a pro. Of course, he *was* a pro— he owned a company that operated twenty-three hotels. One incident like this wouldn't be enough to fluster him.

Imagine if Patrick had left a controlling interest in the *Cora Mae* to her? These urgent discussions would be peppered by her indecision and lack of knowledge, which could only spell disaster for the ship and her crew. She wrapped her arms tightly around her waist.

And where would the money for the repairs come from? Her stomach lurched until she felt nauseous.

Heart thumping against her ribs, she edged toward Luke. "Can I see you for a moment, please?"

He nodded, though clearly distracted, then turned to the captain. "Excuse me a minute."

The room was big enough that they could stand in a corner and not be overheard if they kept their voices low, so they moved to the farthest point from the small group of crew.

"What is it?" he asked, positioning himself so he could watch the others in the room over her shoulder.

"The money." She resisted the urge to wince, and instead stood tall, prepared to meet her responsibilities. "If this will cost more than Captain Tynan's budget, then the expense will have to come from outside of operating costs, yes?"

He shrugged one shoulder, seemingly unconcerned. "Insurance will cover most of it."

"But not all."

"It's hard to say without all the information about what's been damaged," he said, his eyes tracking the movements of the people behind her.

"But from your experience…" She left the sentence hanging and his gaze snapped back to her.

He wrapped a hand around the back of his neck and let out a breath. "From my experience, there will be out-of-pocket expenses. But Marlow Hotels will cover it."

"You only own 50 percent of the *Cora Mae,*" she pointed out, "so you're only responsible for 50 percent of her losses."

The door opened and the head chef, accompanied by the purser, strode across to the table covered with plans. "We've just had a preliminary look at Galley Two."

Luke glanced over, then back to Della. "Can we finish this later? I need to hear their assessment."

He'd said "I," she realized with a resigned sigh. He needed to hear their assessment, not both of them. Which was so obviously true, and pretty much said it all about her potential role in this situation.

She took a step back and pasted on a smile. "Of course. Give my apologies to the group, will you? I have to do a few things. And don't worry about running decisions by me—you just do what you have to do."

Luke frowned, his mouth open as if about to say something, but she slipped out of the room before he could speak. They needed his management skills over at the table. And she needed to be anywhere but here.

Luke found Della on the top deck, her forearms resting on the railing, her gaze on the view of the harbor city sprawled out before them. It had been two hours since their brief discussion about the costs of repairs, and her haunted expression had been in the back of his mind ever

since. It was obvious she didn't have the money to contribute to out-of-pocket expenses, but her despondency
had seemed out of proportion. Perhaps it was her exhaustion coloring her reaction, perhaps there was more to it.
He needed to know.

"Hey, I've been looking for you," he said softly when
he reached her side. He leaned on the railing, their shoulders brushing.

"I've been here, thinking." Her voice sounded as if it
came from far away. She turned and gave him a smile that
didn't reach her eyes. "You were great today."

He shook his head. "I only did some basic first aid. You
were the one who was great."

"I meant after the fire." She turned back to the view, her
expression once again lost, and it nearly broke his heart.

"That was nothing," he said and shrugged. "Just some
organizing."

"To you, maybe. To me it was more."

There was his answer—there *was* more to the situation. And everything inside him yearned to find a way to
make it better for her. To see her happy again.

He wrapped one of her curls around his finger. "Della,
what's going on?"

She turned her back to the railing and crossed her arms
under her breasts. "During the fire, my role was clear. I
was in charge of the first-aid station. You assisted me because I had the expertise. But the business decisions that
followed were your area of expertise. You've lived and
breathed tourism and accommodation facilities most of
your life." She paused and moistened her lips. "If I had the
controlling interest, the best person wouldn't have been
making those decisions. I simply don't have the skill set
to run a ship."

It was what he wanted to hear, exactly the realization he'd hoped she'd come to during their time together, yet the soul-deep loss in her eyes was tearing at him. "Della—"

She rested a finger gently on his lips. "It's not just the decisions, although that's enough on its own. I don't have any available funds to cover the repairs until the insurance kicks in and the extras the insurance won't cover. Or the money for when the next unexpected event occurs. Your company has the resources to run the ship the way it needs to be run. The *Cora Mae* and her crew deserve the stability that only you can provide."

He searched her toffee-brown eyes. "Are you saying you've made a decision?"

"There's really no decision to make—I'll sell some or all of my share of the *Cora Mae* to you. You can have the controlling interest, or own it outright, whichever you prefer. You're the best person for the ship, Luke."

He tightened his grip on the railing till his knuckles went white. This was no victory—he didn't want Della to give up on her dream. Yet it was the outcome he'd been working toward. The outcome the *Cora Mae* needed for stability. Why did it feel so wrong?

He released the railing and pulled her close against him, as if the contact could calm the conflicting thoughts and feelings that were thrashing through his mind and body. "We'll talk about this in the morning. You're exhausted, and that's no state to be making decisions of this magnitude."

"I won't change my mind," she said, her warning tremulous.

"Maybe not, but I refuse to negotiate with someone who's dead on her feet." If nothing else, he needed to be certain he hadn't taken advantage of her state of mind.

"Come back to my cabin, we'll get something to eat, and after a good night's sleep, we'll sort this out."

And after that? A devil on his shoulder prodded. *You'll have finished your business together. Are you ready to let her go?*

His gut fell away, leaving black emptiness. He held Della tighter and willed all the uncertainty away. It was far too soon to think about losing her. Not now that he finally had what he wanted—Della in his arms, in his bed.

Eleven

Della let Luke lead her back to his cabin. He was right—she *was* exhausted, both physically and emotionally. She wouldn't change her mind, but neither did she have the mental space to discuss the details of selling her share tonight.

When they arrived, Luke picked up the phone and ordered dinner. "But don't deliver it to my cabin for forty-five minutes," he said and disconnected.

Della's stomach growled, as if in protest. "Why not as soon as it's ready?"

He took her hand, laced their fingers and led her upstairs. "You need a chance to clean up first. You have soot smudges on your cheeks, and your hair smells of smoke. Everything will seem better after a shower."

"Good point." She'd been drenched with sweat at the first-aid station after the air-conditioning was turned off and she felt grimy. If she hadn't been so tired, getting clean would have occurred to her earlier.

Fingers still entwined, he guided her into the bathroom then turned and took her face in his hands. "Della, I know you haven't wanted me to see your scars, but let me look after you. Trust me, I promise you'll be safe."

Della let out a sigh. She was so tired, and his voice was so sure, so persuasive. And really, what did she have to lose? Their time was over—she'd sell him her share in the morning and he'd leave, probably before lunch tomorrow.

Biting the inside of her cheek to tame the butterflies in her belly, she lifted her shirt over her head and let it fall from her fingers. Then she reached behind her back and unhooked her bra before dropping it, as well. Goose bumps raced across her skin, both from the sudden contact of the cool air, and from fear of his reaction. She stood before him, exposed from the waist up. It was the first time anyone besides her doctors had seen her scarred chest.

She braced herself, heartbeat hard and erratic, and lifted her chin, waiting for his response, hoping it wasn't pity. Praying it wasn't revulsion.

Yet he simply turned her until her back was to him, unzipped her trousers and slid them, with her underpants, down her legs, pausing to let her step out of them. She frowned. Had he seen her chest? She heard the shower start, so turned and saw him pulling his own clothes off. He stepped into the shower, adjusted the water and gently tugged her in with him.

Light-headed with surprise, she looked up into his face for clues, but found only acceptance. He hadn't taken any notice of her scars. All that time worrying, and he was treating her as if she had a normal body. The relief of it brought tears to her eyes, and the weight of everything else that had happened in the previous twelve hours, from the fire to her decision to stop fighting about the ship, pushed the tears down her cheeks.

Under the warm spray, Luke encircled her in his arms and she rested her cheek against his shoulder, not bothering to hide that she was softly crying. He stroked her hair and murmured comforting words above her head.

Patrick had been right—Luke really was a prince among men.

Within a couple of minutes, the tears stopped coming. All the emotion that had bubbled inside her had been released, leaving her almost lethargic, calm.

He reached for a sponge and squirted it with soap that smelled like sandalwood and Luke, and lathered her back in slow, thorough strokes. Then he ran the sponge down her legs and along her arms. The sensation was undemanding, yet its inherent sensuality roused a heat in her bloodstream. He turned her and repeated the soaping process down the front of her arms, across her chest and belly, then along her legs, unhurried, reverentially, as if honoring her body as he cleansed her. Then he lifted her feet, one at a time, and washed beneath them, water running from his hair down his fallen angel's face in rivulets.

Straightening, he rinsed out the sponge and put it back on the end of the bath, then squirted more soap into his hands, rubbed them together until it formed a lather and gently washed her neck, up to her chin and cheeks, then nose and forehead. Della's eyes drifted closed as she allowed herself to be washed, to be nurtured. She'd never loved this man more.

With a hand supporting the nape of her neck, he rinsed her face then placed a chaste, albeit lingering, kiss on her mouth. Emotion welled up from her heart, filling her. Engulfing her. Wrapping her hands behind his neck, she captured him before he could pull away, eliciting more heat from the kiss. Her pulse jerked erratically at the slick feel of his skin against hers, the scrape of his teeth over her bottom lip, the groan that seemed to come from deep in his chest.

Before she became too carried away, she laid a hand on his chest and tore her mouth away. Then, breathing still uneven, she took the sponge, soaped it and began to wash him. She ran it over the golden skin of his back, then across his powerful shoulders. As the soap was rinsed from each area, she kissed the skin she'd cleaned. Down his arms, his chest and the ridges of his abdomen, then lower still, to the apex of his thighs. He was already aroused, and her soaping only increased his reaction, but he didn't move. Just let her continue her path down his muscular legs, washing and leaving a trail of kisses. When she stood, she soaped her hands, as he had done, and washed the planes of a face that had become so dear to her.

She ended as he had done, with a chaste kiss on his mouth, but within moments, the kiss became more. Became everything. The wet slide of his body against hers was a sensual feast, the gentle abrasion of the peaks of her breasts against his hair-roughened chest exquisite. He whispered her name against her lips and the word seemed to reverberate around the shower stall—or perhaps he was repeating it. It barely mattered as long as he kept kissing her.

She reached down, held his fullness and was rewarded with a groan. And suddenly, kissing was no longer enough. Had it ever been?

As if he could read her thoughts, Luke shunted the tap off with an elbow and grabbed a thick white towel from a shelf just outside the shower. He patted her down in the same methodical way he'd washed her, but this time he had a shade less composure as he completed the task. His eyes were darkened, his chest rising and falling rapidly. He quickly rubbed himself over with another towel, then took her hand, leading her to the bed.

When he was sheathed and balancing over her on the mattress, she cupped his face in her hands, making him pause. It was imperative that he know how much tonight had meant to her, that he'd accepted her body so unquestioningly. In one simple shower, he'd given her back her self-worth. Given her back the completeness of her sexuality. The desire in his eyes now, while her imperfect body was on display, was something she never thought she'd see again.

"No matter what happens tomorrow," she said, her voice trembling with emotion, "I'll always remember our lovemaking. I'll always be grateful for what you've done for me."

Luke looked down at Della lying beneath him, trying to think through the fog of desire that filled his head.

Had she just *thanked* him? He was crazy with lust for this woman, and she was *grateful?* As if their time together had been nothing more than pity sex....

It would have been one thing to thank him for looking after her tonight, but it was obvious that wasn't what she meant. His gut clenched tight. Had she simply been dealing with her issues while he'd been so lost in want for her he could barely see straight?

"Let's be clear about one thing," he said fiercely. "This has been about desire and need for me." Brain-melting need. He leaned down, captured her mouth in a fiery kiss, showing her what she did to him, how wild she made him. He lifted one of her legs and hooked it over his elbow, entering her in one smooth stroke. "I've wanted you from the first day," he said through a tight jaw. "I want you even more now."

He'd planned to hold himself in check, to make tonight tender, gentle. But it seemed more imperative now that he not hide his passion. Not hide how close to the edge he was, so she knew that this was *real* between them.

More real than anything else in his life.

She had nothing to feel *grateful* for.

He thrust harder, faster, telling her in plain language the effect she had on him. Her fingers bit into the flesh on his shoulders, arms, wherever she could reach, and he welcomed the tiny points of pain as proof that she was as crazy with lust as he was. Her movements beneath him became more frantic, and he reached down with one hand, found her center and felt tension fill her body then implode around him. Within moments he followed and, as he floated, he had the strange sensation that nothing would be the same ever again.

Nor would he want it to be.

Della blinked as she woke then looked around. Luke was sitting on the side of the bed, already dressed for the day in casual trousers and a polo shirt, and holding a tray with a steaming coffeepot, two glasses of orange juice and an assortment of pastries.

"Morning, sleepyhead," he said and kissed her on the forehead.

"Morning," she said over a muffled yawn. "That coffee smells like heaven."

He held the tray aloft while she sat up and tucked the sheet around herself, then set it on the mattress. "You look like heaven," he said, surveying her with a lazy smile.

A cozy warmth rose inside her, until memories of the day before came flooding back. She was giving in on the

Cora Mae. Luke would be leaving. Probably today. Everything inside her sank low and shivered.

"What time is it?" she said through a dry throat and tried to blink away the grittiness in her eyes. She'd spent much of the night staring into the darkness, contemplating her future, so she hadn't had much sleep.

He poured a coffee and handed it to her. "Six o'clock. I wasn't sure if you were working this morning."

"No, Cal has the morning shift, but I should get up, anyway." She sipped the coffee and closed her eyes as it slid down her throat, the heat calming her a little.

"I've been thinking," he said as he poured another coffee. His posture was relaxed, but there was a spark in his eyes.

Any hope of enjoying what was in all probability their last breakfast together evaporated—his tone said they were talking business. "If this is about me selling you my share, I haven't changed my mind."

"I have an alternative."

She was instantly wary. Luke the businessman wasn't someone to underestimate.

"Tell me." She took an apple pastry from the tray and sampled it.

"I'll be ringing my office this morning and instructing them to put several of my hotels up for sale. I'm going to use that money to start my own cruise line."

Della almost choked on her pastry, and Luke smoothly passed her an orange juice. "Your own line?" she asked when she could talk, trying to comprehend his meaning.

He nodded, as if this was a logical progression from his position only yesterday. "Three ships sounds like a good place to begin," he said, "then I'll grow it from there."

"Three ships," she repeated faintly. All this time she'd been trying to talk him into keeping one, and now he wanted three. His gray gaze was completely serious, perhaps even excited. She could see him making mental calculations as they were talking.

"I might not live full-time on board the way Patrick did, but I'll spend the majority of my time on the ships." He stood and paced around the room, as if the energy of his new plan wouldn't allow him to stay still. "I'll be able to work long hours, just like in the city, but afterward, I'll have all the resources and entertainments of the ship at my disposal. Not to mention days off in various ports."

It was as if their roles had been reversed and now he was selling her on the cruising lifestyle. Della sipped her coffee to give herself a moment to think.

"This is a pretty big turnaround," she finally said.

He sat back on the bed beside her. "The fire gave me a lot to chew over. Crystallized my thinking. The camaraderie of the crew during the fire and its aftermath was impressive, but I've also grown to love the lifestyle of a cruise ship." He took her hand in his. "That's thanks to you."

"I didn't think I was having an impact," she said faintly.

He gave her a crooked smile. "Being on the *Cora Mae* has helped me relax for the first time I can remember. On my deathbed, I don't want to just look back on a career. I want to look back on both a career and a life well lived. No regrets."

He'd never reminded her more of Patrick. She smiled. "I'm starting to see the family resemblance."

Luke's eyes crinkled at the edges. He was obviously pleased by the comparison. "Uncle Patrick lived his life on his own terms, and I bet he had few regrets at the end."

"You're right." She bit down on her lip, wondering how much to say about Patrick's thoughts at the end, but Luke had a right to know. "He said his regrets were mainly about you. Wishing he'd spent more time with you."

Luke blinked hard then looked away. "Patrick often invited me to stay on the *Cora Mae,* and his other ships before this one, but after I took over Marlow Corporation I was always too busy, so I only saw him when he came ashore."

"He knew you loved him. The way he spoke about you, he knew."

He swallowed hard, then cleared his throat. "Thank you for saying that. It means a lot."

"And he'd be thrilled if he knew about your plans."

"Now I understand why he lived here—now I can see what I've been missing—and I don't want to wait. If nothing else, Patrick's death has taught me that life is short."

"I'm happy for you, Luke, I really am." When they'd been in Melbourne she'd thought he was turning from the relaxed man on holidays who'd played mini golf with her into Luke the businessman. But now she could see that he'd managed to integrate all of those parts of himself, perhaps to become the man he'd always meant to be. And it made her heart sing even as it was breaking—the man he was meant to be wasn't a man she could have. He'd been clear that he'd never marry again, and she wouldn't settle for anything less than forever. Being in love and waiting for the inevitable end to their relationship would break her heart by a thousand little cuts. "Seems it's even better timing to sell you my share."

"There's a new offer on the table. I'll convert your half-share of the *Cora Mae* to 20 percent of the new company that will own and run the fleet of ships. You can be a silent partner, or you can have a more active role. It will be up to you."

She put her coffee mug down on the side table before

she spilled it, then checked Luke's face to make sure he
was serious. His gray eyes were dark and steady. Seemed
he was, despite his new offer not adding up. "But 20 percent is a bigger share than what I'd be bringing."

He waved the quibble away and picked up another pastry. "Without you, the new company wouldn't exist. You're
the one who sold me on the concept of cruising. You deserve the extra few percent."

A vision of the life he was suggesting rolled out before
her. She'd be a shareholder in a cruise ship line, as active
as she wanted to be, safeguarding the *Cora Mae*. Having regular business contact with Luke after he'd moved
on from their personal relationship. Having to work with
him, loving him, when she knew he was seeing someone
new. Bile rose in her throat, and she rubbed her arms that
were suddenly cold.

She refused to subject herself to that torture.

Besides, it was time she took control of her own life.
Alone. "Luke, I've been doing some thinking, too." She'd
lain awake most of the night, unable to sleep with all the
thoughts chasing each other in circles in her mind. "I've
realized that I've been hiding on this ship. Patrick was
living the life you're talking about, but I've been staying
here out of fear since my husband died."

He rubbed a thumb over the frown line that had appeared in his forehead. "But you grew up on ships. You
said you wanted to live at sea like your parents."

"I thought I did. But it's one matter for my parents and
Patrick to make those choices. I've been scared of living on land again, which is something entirely different."
Luke's acceptance of her last night had given her the insight into herself. Into the way she'd been hiding. "I realize now that I have to leave and face my fears."

"What exactly does facing your fears entail?" he asked warily.

She pulled her knees up to her chest and wrapped her arms around them tight, as if she could physically control the anxiety that was rising. "Setting up a life on land again. Getting a job in a hospital, finding a place to live. And if you still want it, I'll sell you my share of the *Cora Mae*. You have great plans for her. I know I'll be leaving her in safe hands."

Luke stilled. He'd just decided to live on board…and Della was leaving? He cleared his throat. "You're going?"

"Yes," she said and didn't meet his eyes.

He stood and stalked across the room, a rising blackness filling him. "When?"

"Soon. Now that I've made the decision, there's no point putting it off. I'll talk to Captain Tynan about Dr. Oliver, the doctor who did the locum for me while we were in Melbourne, and if he's happy with her, I'll ring her and see if she wants to apply. It could all be quite soon if things fall into place."

Soon? He was nowhere near ready for her to leave his bed. Especially not after last night. She'd shown him such trust—he'd really thought something had changed between them.

"What if I asked you to stay?" he asked, even though he had to force the words out.

"We were going to end sometime." She shrugged one bare shoulder. "You made it plain on several occasions that you're not looking for anything long-term. Maybe it's better that we end on a high note instead of letting it drag out."

How could she be so calm about this? His heart thundered against his ribs. Did the time they'd spent together mean so little to her? Then he saw her hand tremble as she tucked a curl behind her ear and his chest crushed in on itself. Della Walsh wasn't any calmer about this than he was.

And she was right—he wouldn't marry again. Wouldn't let himself get close enough to another person to rely on them, or trust them implicitly. Why not end it now instead of weeks or months down the line? In fact, if they stayed together and things deteriorated, it would only make their business dealings more awkward. Now was the best time. So why was his stomach clenched hard as a rock, as if he might lose his breakfast at any moment?

"This doesn't feel right." He ran a hand down his face, trying to clear his mind.

She gave him a tremulous smile. "That's because you're too used to getting your own way."

"Perhaps you're right." He sank down on the side of the bed again, ready to face her departure like a man.

"You should never have taught me to tell you to go to hell."

He took her hand and threaded their fingers together. "A mistake I won't repeat." He pulled her hand over and kissed her knuckles. "Della, I want you to know…"

He frowned. How did he tell her what was inside? There weren't words for what he was feeling. Yet he owed it to her to at least try. "I don't want to marry again, or even have something permanent with a woman. But if I did want that—if I was capable of it—it would be you."

A single tear slipped from her eye and curved its way down her cheek before she withdrew her hand from his to wipe it away. "I'd better get going," she said, reaching over the side of the bed for her clothes. "I need to meet with Captain Tynan, and tell Cal, Jody and the rest of the medical team."

Della slipped from his bed, quickly dressed, dropped a

kiss on his cheek then disappeared from his room. From his life. And, with his head a jumble of confusion, Luke watched it happen, powerless to do anything to stop it.

Twelve

Della eased into a chair at the nurses' station and rubbed her eyes before blinking down at the medical chart of the patient she'd just seen in the emergency room. Getting used to shift work again would take some time. Especially when she spent most of the hours when she should be sleeping lying in bed and thinking of Luke. The way he smiled. The way he said her name. The way he made love to her. Sighing, she took a long sip from her water bottle then screwed the cap back on and took a pen from the top pocket of her white coat.

Slipping back into life on land had been unexpectedly simple. The morning she'd told Luke she was leaving—had it really been just five days ago?—she'd also told Captain Tynan. He'd been happy for her to approach Dr. Oliver, who'd covered for her while she was in Melbourne. Jane Oliver had not only been keen to apply for the job but, hoping to make a good impression on the captain, had offered to fill in until the interviews were held, and had caught a flight from Australia to Wellington that afternoon.

While waiting for her replacement to arrive, Della had packed her bags—shipboard life meant she didn't own much—then rung the hospital where she'd worked in Melbourne. They were short-staffed and had been pleased to give her some locum work, starting as soon as she'd like. She'd also called her parents, who'd been thrilled by the chance to see more of her, and offered her a bed for as long as she wanted. Not wanting to give herself thinking time and risk losing her courage, she'd accepted both offers.

Once Dr. Oliver arrived aboard the *Cora Mae,* Della had done a quick hand over and left her in Jody's and Cal's capable hands. She'd already made her farewells to her friends, which she'd tried to handle quickly since she hated goodbyes. There had been a longer, more wrenching goodbye with Luke, though she'd managed not to cry, and hoped she'd at least kept her dignity intact.

Within fourteen hours of telling Luke she was going, she'd left the ship—her home—and caught a flight to Melbourne.

She'd expected the whole process might take weeks to organize, but it had fallen into place with alarming ease. And now here she was, living on terra firma, working at a hospital, just as she'd told Luke she would.

As she read over the notes she'd made in the medical chart, her mobile phone rang. Only a few people had her new number—the hospital, her parents, the crew of the *Cora Mae*...Luke. There were still a few details to sort out with the sale of her share of the ship, so she'd needed to give him a way to get in touch with her, despite knowing that prolonging their contact would only make it harder to get over him.

The new phone hadn't rung often since she'd bought it a few days ago, but each time the ringtone sounded she tensed, wondering if it was Luke. Wishing it was. Hoping it wasn't. Which was crazy—she had to get used to living her life without Luke Marlow in it.

Shaking her head at herself, she checked the number on the screen—it was one of the *Cora Mae*'s phone numbers. Her heart beat double-time as she answered.

"Good morning, Della." The deep rumble of his voice flowed over her, sank down into her heart, where she ached for him, making it difficult to reply.

"Hello, Luke," she finally managed, but the words felt stilted, formal. As if, after all they'd shared, they couldn't have a normal conversation. She turned the swivel chair so she could look out at the hospital parking lot, and tried again. "It's good to hear from you."

"How have you been?"

"Busy. The hospital threw me in the deep end, with shifts in the emergency room starting the day after I came back, but busy is good."

"Have you been okay?" His voice was gentle, probing. She knew what he was asking, of course. The plan to come ashore had been about facing her fears and she loved him all the more for checking.

"You know what? I really have been," she said and bit down on a smile, proud of what she'd achieved. On the flight home from Wellington, she'd been almost sick with worry about how she'd cope back on land, in the town where Shane had been killed, where she'd almost died. It had been hard, but all in all not as bad as she'd built it up to be in her head.

After her first shift, she'd even visited the room where she'd been a patient, and found it no longer held the demons she remembered.

The hardest thing had been the comments about Shane from colleagues who remembered him, telling her how sorry they were. A couple of months ago she wouldn't have been able to bear hearing such things, but now they merely evoked a well of sadness that she guessed would always be there. She'd moved further through her grief than she'd realized. Discovered she was stronger than she'd given herself credit for, and she had Luke to thank for part of that.

"I'm glad to hear it," Luke said.

"How's the *Cora Mae* and the repairs?" she asked brightly, needing to change the subject.

"Everything is on track. We spent an extra couple of nights in Wellington to allow for local tradesmen to work on the repairs, but the captain made up a bit of time across the Tasman Sea. We docked in Melbourne a couple of hours ago."

"I didn't realize." How strange it was to not know the location of the *Cora Mae* after years of being so intimately acquainted with her schedule.

Luke cleared his throat. "Do you have any free time to drop down to the dock today? There are a couple of things I'd like to discuss with you."

Her hands trembled; she dropped the pen on the floor and leaned over to pick it up. "Sure," she said, trying to sound unaffected. As if the world hadn't just wobbled. She checked her watch. "I'm on a night shift and it ends in a couple of hours. Give me time for a shower after I finish and I'll be there."

"I'll see you then." He disconnected and Della was left staring at the phone in her hand, wondering why she'd so easily agreed to see him again so soon. Before she'd developed any distance from her feelings for him.

Given that her heart may never be free of him, perhaps

it was better to get this meeting over and done with so she could go back to building her new life. Perhaps.

Her heart thumping a crazy tattoo, Della stepped into the *Cora Mae's* lobby and glanced around. A few crew members smiled and waved as if she just been ashore for a quick visit, and she waved back. But something was different. There was a hum of tension in the air; too many pairs of eyes were tracking her movements.

She felt Luke's presence before she saw him—a delicious shiver raced across her skin, and everyone else in the lobby seemed to slow to a standstill. The air no longer hummed, it crackled. She turned to see him walking toward her, so tall and broad and all that she wanted…

The aura of confidence that always surrounded him was there, but his gray gaze held a touch of uncertainty. From the corner of her eye she saw a crew member on the grand stairs lean over and whisper something to the person beside him. A sudden sense of déjà vu swamped her, remembering when Luke had boarded the *Cora Mae* on the day she'd first met him, but this time their roles were reversed—he belonged and she was the visitor that people were talking about.

And then Luke reached her and all thoughts of anyone but him flew from her mind. Her hands longed to reach up and stroke the planes of his face that she knew so well. Her lips tingled with the need to touch his. And her heart wanted him to take her in his arms and remove this distance between them.

"Della," he said, his voice a husky whisper. "It's good to see you." He took her hands and leaned in to kiss her cheek. The brief touch of his lips was a moment of heaven, but all too soon he was drawing away, taking a piece of her soul with him.

"Hello, Luke." She withdrew her hands, unable to endure the touch when she couldn't have more.

His gaze dropped to where she'd severed the contact and a faint frown line creased his forehead, but it quickly vanished as he dug his hands into his pockets and flashed her a wholly unconvincing smile. "How about we go somewhere a little more private?"

Given that there seemed to be hundreds of eyes trained on them, she nodded. "Good idea."

As he led her up the grand staircase, he didn't touch her. In fact, he seemed to be deliberately ensuring that not even their arms brushed. She'd been the one to let go of his hand first, yet she couldn't help but wish they still had the closeness where he could drape an arm around her waist, or he would welcome her reaching over and interlacing their fingers.

The stares followed them as they reached the next floor, and the strangeness of the atmosphere finally penetrated the claim Luke had made on her attention. She turned to him, her voice lowered. "Is there something else going on that I don't know about?"

"What do you mean?" he asked, giving nothing away.

She double-checked her surroundings as they set off down one of the promenades. "There seem to be a lot of people watching us."

He shrugged one broad shoulder. "You're more than an average guest," he said, echoing her words to him the day they met.

"So they're watching me because of rumors?" she couldn't resist asking and felt her mouth tug at the corners.

"I'm sure you understand that rumors pass quickly around a ship," he said and guided her to the door to the Blue Moon. She hesitated on the threshold. This wasn't a venue for business discussions, it was for dancing and drinking. The place she'd first felt Luke's arms around her.

He held the door open for her and she tentatively took a step inside—it was empty now, closed until evening. "I thought you might want to talk in an office or a meeting room," she said nervously.

He let the door softly close behind them and flicked a switch. Soft lighting filled the room from above and the twinkling fairy lights in the walls sprang to life. "This isn't about business, and I wanted somewhere I knew we wouldn't be interrupted."

Her heart missed a beat then raced to catch up. "You said on the phone that there were a few details we need to iron out."

"And there are," he said, his voice solemn. He took her hand and led her to the middle of the polished dance floor. "But they're details about us."

Her breath hitched high in her throat. "What do you mean, us?"

"You and me." He met her eyes steadily. "What we have together."

She flinched. Seeing him again, having a conversation like this only emphasized the aching hollow inside her. "Luke, I don't want to start up something again. I can't."

"I'm not talking about starting anything. What's between us isn't over," he said, still holding her hand.

She squeezed her eyes shut for one breath, two, then opened them again and met his gaze. "We've discussed this. If there's no future, then why would we prolong the ending?"

"Tell me something," he said, his hand sliding from her fingers up to her arm. "Is us being apart what you want?"

The imprint of his hand on her arm burned through the

fabric of her sleeve, so she took a step back, once again severing a physical connection.

"Luke, I have to be honest." It seemed there was no other way to circumvent this conversation—the last thing she wanted was to open herself up for more pain, but she couldn't see any other way to make him understand. She crossed her arms tightly under her breasts and exposed her heart. "My feelings for you were more than I expected. I *can't* see you anymore. Please don't ask me to—it would be emotional suicide."

"Because your feelings were more than you expected or wanted," he clarified, saying each word slowly, carefully.

"Please don't make this worse." Her voice wobbled, the final indignity. She turned to the door, escape the only refuge remaining. "If there's nothing to discuss about the *Cora Mae* or the sale of my share, then—"

He stepped around so he was again in her line of vision, his face pale. "Della, I asked you to come today so I could tell you how grateful I am that you spent the time showing me the *Cora Mae* and convincing me to keep her cruising. That time you invested changed my life."

She swallowed the sudden constriction in her throat. "I'm glad for you, Luke, but—"

"What I didn't realize before you left was that the change was in more than just my opinion of the ship. I know now that the lifestyle I was so impressed with was only partly about the ship and cruising. It was also about you."

"Luke—" she said, praying her tone was warning, but knowing it was probably pleading.

"The ship was different when you left—" he took an infinitesimal step closer "—as if you took something with you. It might be greedy but, Della, I want it all."

His heart was in his eyes, and that stunned her more

than anything he could say. For a charged moment, she didn't respond. "All?" she finally said, her voice an octave higher than normal.

"I want the ships *and* you." He took another step closer, till she could feel the body heat emanating from him, but he didn't try to touch her this time. "And if I had to choose just one, it would be you."

Something fluttered in the pit of her belly and she placed a hand over her stomach to calm it. "You'd give up the ships after rearranging your life to have them?"

He didn't hesitate. "No question. I love you, Della. I was in love with you before you left but didn't understand." He speared his fingers through his hair. "Or perhaps I didn't *want* to understand."

"What does that mean to you? For us?" she asked warily.

"It means I'm abandoning my stupid ideas about never marrying or letting anyone close. Once you were gone I realized that all I really need is you." He tucked a curl behind her ear. "I thought I couldn't trust anyone. I guess I was expecting people to abandon me, not stand by me in the tough times, but that's not what you're about. Your strength in moving on after such an awful past showed me up for what I was—an emotional coward. You've inspired me to want to face life fully. Hell, I want to grab life and live it to the hilt. With you."

She tried to blink away the prickling burn behind her eyes but it wouldn't ease. "Oh, Luke, I love you, too. So much."

A shudder ripped through his body, and then he was there, hauling her against him, holding her close. She wrapped her arms around him, not sure she'd ever let him go. Luke *loved* her. It felt magical, a miracle, and she laughed even as the tears she'd been holding in check began to slip down her cheeks.

"I love you with everything inside me," he murmured beside her ear, then pulled back and tenderly brushed her tears away with his thumbs. "Marry me. I know you're keen to try living on land, and I promise that if you say yes, I won't tie you down. We can live our lives ashore, or on the *Cora Mae,* or any combination you want. Nothing is more important than you."

Her heart flipped over in her chest. It was even more than she'd dreamed of. "Yes," she said and heard the tears in her voice. "To everything, yes."

She twined her arms up behind his neck and kissed him, and knew she'd come home. If they never moved from this spot again, she wouldn't mind—she could stay here in Luke's arms, losing herself in his kiss forever.

But Luke eventually pulled away, slipping a hand into his pocket and retrieving a small velvet box. Trembling, she took the box and opened it to find a solitaire diamond sparkling up at her from its white-gold band. A tear slipped down her cheek—his choice of something simple and classic showed how well he knew her.

"It's perfect," she breathed.

He smiled into her eyes. "It's you." He took the box from her hand and slipped the ring on her finger. She reached up on tiptoes and kissed him again, but before they became carried away Luke wrenched himself back, his breath coming hard and a reluctant smile on his lips. Then he strode over to the door and knocked loudly three times. The doors burst open and people flowed into the room, throwing streamers and releasing balloons. Della was stunned—all she could do was watch the commotion around her and try not to gape. A massive congratulatory banner appeared from above, and a loud chorus of cheers went up.

Jody made her way through the crowd and, grinning widely, drew Della into a hug. "I knew you and Luke belonged together. I just knew it."

Before Della could reply, Jody was edged out of the way by Max, who also hugged her and whispered, "You know where to find me if things don't work out with Marlow." With a wink, he was gone.

Della still hadn't caught her breath when Cal hugged her and then shook Luke's hand, congratulating them both. Roxie Appleby dragged Luke closer and linked his hand to Della's. "I couldn't be happier for you two," she said, her voice thick with emotion.

Della watched Roxie move away though the crowd, still marveling at the scene around her. She spotted Captain Tynan raising a glass in her direction and she waved. One of the ship's singers had started to croon a love ballad, and more people were still pouring in through the doors.

She turned to Luke and whispered in his ear, "So this is why everyone was watching me when I arrived?"

He chuckled, and drew her against him. "After you left, I was dragged aside by crew member after crew member. For two days they each had their say about what an idiot I'd been."

Della coughed out a laugh and opened her mouth to protest, but he silenced her with a finger on her lips. "They were right. And the only way to get them to stop haranguing me was to tell them I was going to get you back. Once they heard that, the story traveled around the ship like wildfire, and they all wanted to be involved. My only stipulation was they gave us absolute privacy until you'd made your decision."

"I appreciate that," she said, imagining the horror of

having a private moment like they'd shared play out in front of hundreds of people.

Luke shrugged his broad shoulders. "If you'd had an audience, you'd have felt pressured to say yes, and I wanted to be one hundred percent sure you wanted me for me."

"And what do you think now?" she asked.

He squeezed her a little tighter and rested his forehead on hers. "It's a miracle, but it appears you do love me."

"You'd better believe it," she said and smiled up at him.

When Luke dragged her away from the others and gathered her close for another kiss, she was dimly aware of the hooting from the crew, but the spectacle around her soon melted away and she became lost in the arms of the man she loved.

* * * * *

MILLS & BOON®

Want to get more from Mills & Boon?

Here's what's available to you if you join the exclusive **Mills & Boon eBook Club** today:

✦ *Convenience – choose your books each month*
✦ *Exclusive – receive your books a month before anywhere else*
✦ *Flexibility – change your subscription at any time*
✦ *Variety – gain access to eBook-only series*
✦ *Value – subscriptions from just £1.99 a month*

So visit **www.millsandboon.co.uk/esubs** today to be a part of this exclusive eBook Club!

914_ST_2

MILLS & BOON®

Why shop at millsandboon.co.uk?

Each year, thousands of romance readers find their
perfect read at millsandboon.co.uk. That's because
we're passionate about bringing you the very best
romantic fiction. Here are some of the advantages
of shopping at www.millsandboon.co.uk:

* **Get new books first**—you'll be able to buy your
  favourite books one month before they hit
  the shops

* **Get exclusive discounts**—you'll also be able to buy
  our specially created monthly collections, with up
  to 50% off the RRP

* **Find your favourite authors**—latest news,
  interviews and new releases for all your favourite
  authors and series on our website, plus ideas for
  what to try next

* **Join in**—once you've bought your favourite books,
  don't forget to register with us to rate, review and
  join in the discussions

Visit **www.millsandboon.co.uk**
for all this and more today!